Autumn Skies & Pumpkin Pies

The Coleman Series

Katie Winters

Chapter One

It was the first day of November on the island of Martha's Vineyard, and a blisteringly cold rush of air crashed into the coastal home outside Oak Bluffs, making the windowpanes shiver. Meghan was up in the attic, the chilliest place in the entire house, digging through crates of Christmas, Thanksgiving, Easter, and summertime decorations— her brow furrowed. To her left was the box of Halloween decor she'd just removed from the exterior of the house— plastic jack-o-lanterns, a cute little witch with a green face and a wart on her nose, and candy corn lights. Last night, trick-or-treaters had come in droves, jumping out of their parents' cars in princess, superhero, witch, or silly costumes, high on sugar, crying out to Meghan, "Trick or treat!" But when she and her husband, Hugo, had woken up that morning, Hugo had opened the drapes and announced, "Autumn's over, honey. Winter came early."

Meghan loved holidays. Her holiday decoration collection was a testament to that, to her belief that every day was worth celebration and a little bit of pizzazz.

Gingerly, she raised the Thanksgiving decoration box from the corner and replaced it with the Halloween box, acknowledging the transition of seasons. She was forty-seven years old, headed toward fifty, but she had her health; she had her husband and her two wonderful children, Eva and Theo. She didn't need anything else.

That's when she saw the box. It was shoved into the back row of holiday boxes; its edges crinkled with a heavy skin of dust all over it. What made it remarkable was the faded ribbon around it, ornate and sophisticated. More than that: Meghan wasn't sure she'd ever seen that box before. This wasn't strange, she supposed. Although she felt her life was meticulously curated, and she prided herself on her organizational skills, it was more than possible she'd forgotten a random box up in the attic. As she reached for it, suppressing a sneeze from the dust, she guessed it was an old present she'd once wrapped and forgotten— something for her sister, Oriana or even for their mother before her death.

"Meghan? Where are you?" Hugo's warm voice swelled through the house. He'd been in his study, working, and she'd decided not to disturb him as she took down the Halloween decorations and set up the Thanksgiving ones. She'd wanted it to be a surprise.

Abandoning the mysterious box and the Thanksgiving decor, Meghan headed for the attic ladder and called back. "I'm in the attic!"

Down in the hallway, Hugo popped out of their bedroom, wearing a crooked smile. He was five years older than her, fifty-two, but was healthy and trim from his daily runs, with a mostly gray head of curly hair that Meghan adored. Sometimes it was hard for Meghan to believe they'd done so much life together, that they'd raised two children, that they'd traveled all over the world.

"What are you doing up there?" Hugo teased her.

Meghan laughed. "Now that I'm covered in dust, I'm asking myself the same thing."

"Do you need help?"

Meghan turned and stepped lightly down the ladder, abandoning the shadows and entering the warmth of the hallway below. "Not in the slightest. You're going running?"

Hugo was wearing a pair of running pants, a thick hoodie, and a big hat. "I have to get used to running in the cold one of these days."

"You're a brave man." Meghan sauntered toward him, rolled up onto her toes, and kissed him softly on the lips. As their kiss broke, the doorbell rang downstairs. "Who could that be?"

"I have a guess."

Meghan and Hugo padded down the staircase, eyes to the front window as Oriana leaped from her car and walked gingerly up the ice-glazed sidewalk. This was typical Oriana-Meghan behavior: frequently, they stopped by one another's homes without calling or texting first, as though they still lived down the hall from one another and were popping in and out of each other's bedrooms. Just before Oriana rang the bell, Meghan opened it, and Oriana collapsed over her in a chilly hug.

"Winter is early!" she cried.

"I caught Meghan up in the attic," Hugo said. "Her lips were blue."

Meghan swatted him. "You should talk. You're the one going on a run!"

Oriana's eyes were saucers. "I say this every year, Hugo, but you're insane."

Hugo saluted her on his way out the door, fitting his earphones into his ears and disappearing down the road. For a moment, Oriana and Meghan watched him out the window, the long lope of his stride, until he disappeared around a line of trees.

"I wish I had half his discipline," Oriana joked. Meghan wanted to point out that Oriana's discipline was simply directed in a different place, that she was a killer art dealer who frequently handled million-dollar-plus deals. But before she could, Oriana interrupted to say, "I heard a rumor Eva's coming back tonight?"

Meghan's heart lifted. "Yes! The plane lands at Logan at four, and then she and Finn are driving back to the island. They're coming for dinner tonight, as is Theo."

"You must be over the moon," Oriana breathed.

"They weren't gone very long," Meghan said. "But you know how I get when my babies aren't both on the island."

"I feel the same," Oriana assured her.

Meghan led Oriana to the kitchen, where she put a kettle on the stovetop and searched through boxes of tea— ginger for Oriana and green for Meghan. Eva and Finn had been on a trip to Italy, where they'd celebrated six years of their relationship, a gorgeous milestone for two people on their way to the rest of their lives together.

"I was thinking," Meghan began, as the kettle bubbled and spat, "that Eva started dating Finn at the same age I was when I started dating Hugo."

"Yes, but you already had two kids by the time you were twenty-six," Oriana pointed out.

Meghan wrinkled her nose and spoke in a silly whisper. "I know better than to push for grandchildren. Eva is finding herself, you know."

"Don't you feel like their generation is always trying to find themselves?" Oriana asked. "When we were that age, we charged into life, made tons of mistakes, and figured it out as we went. I can't remember sitting down and actually asking myself, 'who am I?'"

Meghan giggled as she poured hot water. "I can't imagine you slowing down long enough for that. You started your career and your family at the same time! In New York City, no less."

"Sometimes Reese and I look at each other and shake our heads," Oriana said. "We were crazy to think it would work."

"But it did," Meghan reminded her.

"But yours did, too." Oriana blew on the steam over her tea. "You knew you wanted to be a trader since you were a teenager. You sat in Dad's study for hours, asking him questions, studying him."

"You must have thought I was so lame," Meghan said.

"I definitely did," Oriana teased. "But how many women can say they taught their husbands their trade rather than the other way around?"

Meghan smiled inwardly, secretly very proud of that. At the age of twenty, when she and Hugo had officially begun dating, she'd already carved out a successful career for herself in day trading, selling stocks and bonds back in the pre-internet age. On their first date, Hugo had been flabbergasted with what he called her "brilliance," saying, "I feel so lame. I'm just a manager at a coffee shop, thinking about going back to school."

It had taken Hugo about six months to ask Meghan to teach him how to trade. By then, of course, Meghan had

Katie Winters

already gotten pregnant with Eva. They'd needed the money.

"How is work going?" Oriana asked, hands wrapped comfortably around her mug of tea.

"Better than ever," Meghan answered, trying to suppress a smile. "Hugo and I have a quiet competition going. And we're trading off teaching Theo the ropes, as well."

Meghan explained her plans for the next few hours: that she wanted to decorate the house for the Thanksgiving season, set the table with their mother's china, and prepare a feast for her children. Oriana showed photographs of the art project she, Reese, and her grandson, Benny, had completed that morning— little clay pots they'd fired and painted. Benny's was a thick, bulky rock, while Oriana's was sleek, painted turquoise, something you could have picked up in a tourist shop.

"Have you ever considered making your own art and selling it?" Meghan asked, flicking through the photographs on Oriana's phone.

"Gosh, no," Oriana said. "I'm not the artist in the family. That's Alexa."

Meghan gave her a rueful look. "You've spent your life championing other people's art. That means you have a real, artistic eye."

Oriana rarely got embarrassed, which was why Meghan was surprised to see her cheeks flash with pink. She took her phone back and pocketed it, drawing her blonde hair behind her ears.

"I forgot to ask you," Oriana said. "Do you know what you're wearing to the wedding this weekend?"

"I'm struggling between two dress options," Meghan

6

explained, allowing Oriana to change the subject. "An ochre and a forest green."

"You look fantastic in forest green," Oriana said, worrying her lower lip. "I need to get organized. That wedding is going to be fancy, and I have to look the part."

Meghan laughed. "Did you see how panicked Charlie looked last week?"

Oriana's eyes widened. "I get it. Wedding stress is killer. On top of that, Sheila is his first daughter to get married. I'm sure he's going through about a thousand different emotions per day."

"I have a feeling Shawna is keeping everybody afloat," Meghan said, speaking of Charlie's wife.

"That doesn't mean she's not going crazy, too. But like most women, she's better at hiding it," Oriana said knowingly.

After she finished her tea, Oriana rattled off a list of everything else she had to do that day, including a stop at the pharmacy and the grocery store. Meghan walked her to the door, wrapped her in a hug, and told her to drive safely. As Oriana backed out of the driveway, Meghan kept her eyes on the foggy horizon, hunting for some sign of her long-limbed husband. But often, when he went running, he committed to ten miles or more— which meant he was still out there somewhere, his heart pumping, his rock music blaring in his ears. She made a mental note to make sure his running clothes were warm enough; maybe they needed to go shopping for more layers.

Meghan had decided to make Eva's favorite meal: a Cajun Seafood Pasta recipe that Meghan had mastered over the years, frequently pulling it out to help Eva through emotional eras of her life, through fights with friends or previous breakups with high school boyfriends. She wanted to use it to remind Eva just how wonderful home life could be, especially after her magical time in Italy. "There's no place like home," Meghan imagined her saying.

Meghan returned to the attic to fetch the Thanksgiving decorations, thinking she could set up a few things here and there before she got started on dinner. Back in the dusty-filled room, her shoulders tightened with the chill, and she grabbed the box quickly, shuffling back toward the ladder. But as she went, her eyes scanned that dusty box, the mysterious one with the ribbon around it, and she grabbed it and stacked it on top of the Thanksgiving cornucopia. Whatever it was, she would deal with it now.

With the ladder set back in place, Meghan carried the boxes to her study, which she'd decorated exclusively with her own taste in mind: floral wallpaper, a thickly cushioned couch the color of mustard yellow. It was here she conducted her business; here, she made her money. And as she dropped down on the mustard couch and gingerly removed the top of the ribboned box, she thought abstractly, *Wow, how lucky am I?*

The box was filled with thin, yellowed pages, upon which were scrawled many lines of handwriting Meghan didn't recognize. Meghan jumped through initial explanations: that this was a family member's handwriting, perhaps her mother's sisters, or that Theo's ex-girlfriend had written him numerous notes that he'd shoved into the attic, unable to throw away. But Theo was only twenty-four, and these letters were clearly older than that.

Her heart burning with curiosity, Meghan unfurled the top letter and read the salutation at the top: *My darling Hugo.*

Immediately, Meghan dropped the paper, watching as it floated like a dead leaf to the ground. She had the sudden sensation that she was no longer supplied with the right amount of oxygen, which in turn would trigger a fainting spell to the carpeting.

After a labored breath, Meghan forced herself to read the first few lines of the next letter in the pile.

My darling Hugo,

You can't imagine how little I sleep these days, knowing the future I'd thought was bound to be ours is now at risk. All my life, I'd longed for a love like ours— a love that allows me to float away from the horrors of my real day-to-day. When I first met you, I knew everything was about to change.

You told me you have to think and that you need space. But Hugo, you're the only person in the world I don't need space from. I want to sit with you, scream at you, allow you to scream at me; I want us to unburden ourselves from our own emotions and come clean.

But most of all, I want to prove the depths of my love for you. I want you to know just how much I'm willing to do to keep our love alive. I cannot accept that our engagement might be over. I need to believe in our future. I need you.

Meghan blinked up from the letter. Tears streamed from her eyes, blurring her study, and dotting the note below. Her thoughts shimmering with panic, she went through thousands upon thousands of conversations with Hugo over the years, trying to drum up a memory in which he'd told her about a previous engagement. There was nothing.

Feeling like a masochist, bent on destroying her own heart, Meghan continued to read the letters. They were

all addressed to Hugo, and they spoke of a profound relationship, a harsh disagreement, a broken engagement—
and finally, a threat.

My darling Hugo,

*I hear you loud and clear. Most of my letters have
remained unanswered, and I feel as though I'm screaming
over an empty abyss and hearing only my own echoes
coming back. The only thing keeping me from hating you
is that I love you so much.*

But now, I must set a boundary.

*If I don't hear back from you, you will never see me or
hear from me again. The love we once had for one another
won't matter in the slightest. It will be as though we never
knew each other. And, Hugo, I will teach myself to hate
you. I will not uphold a single memory with you. It will be
as though all the love we shared never existed.*

*I implore you to listen to reason, to come to me and say
what I know you feel— that you love me so completely and
that you don't want what we have to die.*

This is your final chance.

Suddenly, Meghan heard the creak of footsteps on the
staircase and the warm call of her husband. "Meghan? I'm
home!" His voice was clipped short, his breath ragged
after his run. Meghan staggered forward, allowing the box
of letters to tumble from her lap and onto the floor. Her
vision filled with dark spots, as though she was about to
faint.

"Meghan?" Hugo called again.

Meghan wrapped her hands around her throat and
stared out the window, listening as the harsh winter
winds crashed against the sturdy coastal home— the
house she and Hugo had bought so many years ago when
their love had been the only thing Meghan had fully

understood. Had she been a fool? It felt as though the foundation upon which she'd built her love for Hugo was now filled with mold, crumbling. She had the sudden desire to kick it and watch it completely fall apart.

"I'm here!" Meghan's voice was shaky as she called back to him, feeling him move about the second floor.

Hugo walked toward her study door, and Meghan's veins were shot through with adrenaline and fear. It was as though the bogeyman lurked in the hallway, ready to nab her.

"Are you working?" Hugo asked.

"Um. Yeah."

Hugo's voice quivered with confusion. "Are you okay?" He paused. "Did something happen with Oriana?"

Hugo was probably referring to Meghan and Oriana's recent "confusing" time, in which Meghan had thought Oriana was avoiding her, and Oriana had simply been dealing with a ravenous blackmailer bent on destroying her art career. It had been a misunderstanding, to say the least, one she and Oriana had easily repaired.

"No. She just had to go to the store," Meghan responded.

Hugo shifted his weight on the other side of the door. "Can I come in?"

"No!" Meghan's voice was high-pitched. "I mean, I'm really in the middle of something right now. Why don't you go shower? I'll finish up here and start dinner."

"All right. Just let me know if you need anything," Hugo said quietly, his ego damaged. He knew her well and could feel something was wrong, something he couldn't put his finger on.

But, as Hugo went to their bedroom and started the

shower, Meghan stewed in fear and anger that threatened to fill her chest and drown her. She'd known and loved Hugo Porter for twenty-seven years of her life. She'd given him everything— every detail of her past, every opinion she'd ever held. Why hadn't he thought to tell her about his profound romance?

And then, a thought struck her like a hammer to the head.

Was it possible Hugo had dated this woman while married to Meghan? Was it possible he'd betrayed her?

Chapter Two

The White Whale Bookstore was Oak Bluffs' only indie bookstore, located in a quaint Victorian home painted a soft lavender blue. Daniel Bloom rented the space from the owners, who were self-described 'literary lovers,' for a monthly rate he understood to be much less than most other rentals downtown. Even still, Daniel struggled to make ends meet— often kicking himself for ever opening a bookstore in the first place. He loved books, but it seemed, more and more, that the rest of the world did not.

Lucky for him, a novelist named Layla Johnson currently resided on Nantucket, the island to the east. On a recent trip to Martha's Vineyard, she'd strolled into his bookstore, and Daniel had leaped at the chance to talk to her, explaining he'd fallen in love with her writing as a younger man and followed her career obsessively. She was in her mid-fifties, he thought, just a little bit younger than he was, but with a dense career behind her, one that should have made her a lot more arrogant than she was. When he sheepishly asked if she would be willing to do a signing at his bookstore, she'd agreed, explaining she'd never fallen in love with a part of the world more and wanted to give back to these islands. "People need local bookstores," she'd said. "They're essential parts of communities. And I've hated watching so many of them close over the years."

It was November 3rd, a Friday, and Daniel was setting up for the book signing. He positioned a long table near the window, upon which he stacked numerous copies of Layla's novels. According to a social media event he'd made, at least forty-five people planned to be in attendance, and he hoped they would bring their friends. More than that, people were out and about on the sidewalk, and he wrote: Layla Johnson - Book Signing! on a sign in chalk, hoping that would lure more people in. Christmas was around the corner; maybe people would buy presents along with a few Layla Johnson signed copies?

Layla arrived twenty minutes before the signing was set to begin. She had dark reddish-brown hair and an honest, nervous smile, and she perused Daniel's collection before setting up at the signing table, explaining she was living at The Copperfield House right now, teaching a writing seminar.

"I'm jealous of your students," Daniel said with a sigh.

"Did you ever study writing?" Layla asked, her hands around a Jane Austen classic.

"I took a few classes in college," Daniel explained. "I think I was too arrogant. I couldn't take criticism, and I found another path."

"Taking criticism is tough," Layla said. "I still struggle with it."

"I can't imagine anyone criticizing your work," Daniel said. "You're Layla Johnson!"

"I'm an imperfect person with many problems," Layla corrected. "Like everyone else."

Just as Daniel had hoped, the forty-five people who'd said they were coming on social media brought their friends, and very soon, the bookstore was full. A line snaked around the space and out the door, with numerous Layla Johnson fans shivering outside, hands shoved in pockets, talking excitedly. A thick ceiling of clouds kicked snowflakes to the ground, and Daniel put on Christmas songs, hoping it would remind people to buy presents.

After Layla signed books for a full two hours (incredible, Daniel thought), she suggested she could do a reading from one of her more recent books for those still in the store. People leaped at the chance, either standing toward the back or actually sitting on the floor in front of Layla's table. Daniel was behind the cash register, alternating between listening to Layla and considering what kind of boon this day had been for his bookstore's future. Bit by bit, he felt the panic and anxiety dissolving from his chest, and he took deep, powerful breaths. Maybe everything was going to be okay.

But just as he allowed himself a moment of peace, everything fell apart again.

The door burst open, and an old woman appeared. She wore only a dirty white dressing gown, and her white hair was unkempt, like a scarecrow's. She was very frail, her mouth a scab of chapped lips. Immediately, Layla stuttered over her words, and everyone in the crowd turned to stare at her. Daniel felt as though he was having an out-of-body experience. How was this happening?

Daniel bolted around the side of the cash register and

placed his hand gently on his mother's shoulder just as she cried out in a harsh, rattly voice, "Danny? Where the heck is the remote?"

The crowd stared at Daniel and his mother, Pam, with horrible, suspicious eyes. She'd interrupted Layla Johnson's terrific reading and torn a hole through their perfect Friday afternoon. Daniel raised a shaking hand and locked eyes with Layla, saying, "Please, go on." Layla got the hint and bowed her head again, returning her fans to her fictional world. Meanwhile, Daniel led his mother around the cash register and into the back room, alternating between fuming and feeling frightened. He placed his mother in a cushioned reading chair in the office, one he often sat in to peruse potential buys, and checked her vitals. Her heartbeat was, as always, soft and dangerously slow, but her color was all right. Her eyes were rabid, proof of her confusion. A part of him wanted to curl up against her and cry, if only to remind her that she was his mother; she was supposed to take care of him. But those days were over now. The roles had been reversed.

"Mom? Why did you leave home?" Daniel asked quietly, not wanting to frighten her or anger her.

Pam sucked in her cheeks. "I don't know why a woman can't go where she pleases. It isn't the nineteenth century anymore, you know."

Daniel sighed and rubbed the back of his neck, then stood to turn on the electric water kettle to make her a mug of tea. As it boiled, his mother blathered on about something that enraged her, something that didn't make any sense to Daniel, as Daniel removed his phone from his pocket and dialed Cindy.

Cindy answered groggily on the fourth ring. "Hello?" Her voice was thick with mucus.

"Hi, Cindy." Daniel tried his best to keep his anger at bay. "My mother is here."

Cindy coughed into the phone, making Daniel's ears ring. "Beg your pardon?"

Was she being purposefully obtuse? "My mother is here. You were supposed to be watching her?"

Cindy yelped. "Oh my gosh. She was just here!"

Daniel closed his eyes as waves of annoyance crashed against him like the waves off the Nantucket Sound. "Did you fall asleep again?"

Cindy was quiet. Daniel hated himself in this moment, feeling as though he was a high school principal trying to shame a student. But Cindy was a forty-five-year-old out-of-work nurse who'd agreed to sit with his mother at their home while Daniel was at the bookstore. He understood how boring that task was; he'd done it plenty of times himself. But didn't he pay her enough not to sleep on the job?

"I'm so sorry, Dan," Cindy said, using an abbreviation for Daniel's name that Daniel really didn't like. "It won't happen again."

Daniel stuttered with disbelief, trying to drown his anger. He really couldn't afford to fire Cindy. She was the only person with the time and inclination to sit at home with his mother, and with the holiday season coming up, he needed her more than ever.

"I'll come to the shop and get her right away," Cindy said, her voice hardened with resolve.

"Can you bring her coat? And shoes. She has two different ones on right now," Daniel said, eyeing the right-foot of his mother's tennis shoe and the left-foot of her saddle shoe, which she'd previously worn to church before the dementia had gotten too bad.

After Daniel hung up the phone, his mother glowered at him. "You know I don't like it when Lisa stays out too late."

Daniel struggled to ignore this— a horrific reminder of the past. It felt like a piece of shrapnel shoved through his heart.

"She'll be home soon, Mom," Daniel said instead. "Why don't you drink your tea? I'll turn on the television for you."

Daniel set up his MacBook in front of her and put on her old favorite TV show, *The Golden Girls*. Immediately, his mother's face became slack, and her eyes twitched as she followed the women across the screen. Hoping she was all right alone for the moment, Daniel hurried back into the bookstore to listen to the final few paragraphs of Layla's reading. As she finished, he touched his cheeks to find them wet with tears.

Wonderfully, many of the people who'd stayed to listen to Layla read decided to hang around the store, drink coffee, eat the baked goods Daniel had set out, and buy more books. Daniel allowed his heart to fill with gratefulness as he watched the revenue of the day go up and up and up. And in between the heads of the customers who approached the register, he finally spotted Cindy, bustling in from the snow, her face stricken. Perhaps because of her nerves about potentially losing her job, she tried to burst through the customers to talk to Daniel, to apologize again, but Daniel gave her a dark look and said very quietly, "She's in the back. Wait with her until I'm finished here." He didn't want to frighten anyone off.

After the bookstore cleared, Layla approached him

with her coat on, her eyes heavy. Under her breath, she said, "Is everything okay, Daniel?"

Maybe because Daniel had read so many of Layla's books over the years, he had a false sense of her knowing him and visa versa. He nearly burst with the story: that his mother's dementia had destroyed her, that his life was now filled only with her health problems and the failing bookstore.

"My mother is sick," he said simply, trying to make the fact of it smaller than it was. "It's why I came back to Martha's Vineyard in the first place. To take care of her."

"That's so kind of you," Layla said, her brow furrowed.

"Her nurse fell asleep," he explained, "and she must have snuck out. It's miraculous she still knows the way to the store."

"That's proof of the power of a mother's love, right?" Layla suggested. "She knows right where you are, no matter what."

Daniel wanted to laugh at that. He imagined himself falling to the floor, crying with laughter. But Layla Johnson didn't know the truth: that before Pam's diagnosis, she'd been one of the most cruel and manipulative people in the world. He still woke up sweating with memories of what she'd said to him as a kid. No, she'd never been physically violent, besides a few smacks here and there. But words had a way of lodging themselves into your psyche and affecting you long after.

Daniel thanked Layla again for her help and watched as she stepped out into the November snow, disappearing around the corner to fetch her car. He then counted to ten before he headed back to find his mother asleep in the reading chair and Cindy captivated with *The Golden Girls.*

"This show is hilarious," Cindy said, trying to make peace. "I understand why your mom loves it."

Daniel decided to close the bookstore early, send Cindy back home, and walk his mother the three blocks back to the house in which she'd raised him and his sister, Lisa. It was a three-bedroom, two-story house with a tiny backyard that had once flourished with Pam's garden but was now unkempt and brown. The front door was unlocked, presumably because Cindy had forgotten to lock it, but Daniel decided not to bother himself with getting angry about that. There was so much else to consider.

Daniel drew his mother a bath, hoping to warm her up. It was six in the evening, and his stomach rumbled with hunger, which he would eventually satiate with a microwavable meal— maybe chicken penne or lasagna. It had been a long time since he'd eaten something that didn't taste like sand.

With his mother in the bath, Daniel set up a speaker to play classical music, which often calmed her. He then sat in the hallway, in sight of his mother, never far, just in case something happened. He'd read once that you could drown with just a teaspoon of water.

As he sat glumly, thinking about the wide expanse of emotions from yet another day in his life, his phone buzzed with a text from his wife.

> GINA: Hey. I still haven't heard from you about the papers. It's been six months, Daniel, for crying out loud. I, for one, want to move on. Don't you?

Chapter Three

The ferry from Martha's Vineyard to Nantucket lasted approximately one hour and ten minutes. It was Saturday morning, four hours before they were needed at the welcoming reception prior to Sheila and Jonathon's wedding, and Meghan was wrapped in her winter coat in the café of the ferry, peering through the thick plastic glass at an ocean that frothed angrily. Beneath it, she could feel the immensity of an underwater world nobody quite understood, thousands and thousands of leagues of underwater animals and lost shipwrecks and danger. She now thought of her husband that way— a man she'd assumed, for so many years, to be something she'd now learned he was not. It wasn't smart to underestimate the ocean. Perhaps the same thing could be said about those you loved and their capacity to destroy you.

"Mom! Did you want milk in your coffee?" Eva called from the café counter, waving a red glove.

Meghan blinked out of her reverie, trying and failing to smile at Eva. At twenty-six, she looked remarkably like Meghan had at her age, and the result was striking, as though Meghan looked through a portal that served as a time machine.

"Um. No thanks," Meghan offered, trying to tell herself to act normally, to be the mother Eva and Theo knew. But each time she tried to put on a brave face, pain rocketed through her heart and shot through her limbs.

Eva returned to the table with two mugs of coffee and nodded her head toward the corner, where her boyfriend, Finn, Theo, and Hugo were conversing about sports.

"I always think they'll run out of topics," she said. "But they never do."

Meghan blew over the top of her coffee, eyeing Hugo, remembering the love she'd once felt for his crooked smile and the sharp crow's feet that extended from his eyes.

"Mom?" Eva's voice was delicate and sensitive as Meghan forced herself to look at her daughter. She remembered how she'd been at that age, twenty-six, with two young children and a husband she'd thought was her entire universe. Had she been so wrong?

"Are you okay?" Eva pressed quietly. "You've been so quiet since I got home from Italy."

Meghan sipped her coffee and crossed her arms over her chest. "I'm fine, honey. Just dealing with some work stress right now."

"Oh no. Why didn't you say anything before?" Eva glanced toward her father and brother before adding, "Is it something Dad or Theo could help you with?"

Anger spiked through Meghan's chest, which attempted to calm with a sip of coffee. She wanted to remind her daughter that it had been Meghan, in fact, who'd taught Hugo how to day trade— that she required no assistance from any backstabbing man, nor any man at all.

"I know you've helped Dad so much," Eva hurried to add, as though she could read the horror in Meghan's eyes. "He'd love to return the favor."

Meghan smiled, feeling herself show too many of her teeth. "It'll all work out, honey. Besides, it's a wedding. I'll cheer up in no time." Meghan had never heard herself utter such a big lie.

As the ferry sidled up against the Nantucket port, Meghan, Hugo, Theo, Eva, and Finn returned to their SUV. Meghan sat up front, less than a foot from her darling husband, who tried for the twelfth time that day to hold her hand. She shook him off and stared out the window. Probably because so many others were in the car, Hugo didn't press the issue, although she felt his sidelong glance, his curiosity and confusion.

"Here we go!" Hugo said as they drove off the ferry, heading toward the gorgeous, five-star Wauwinet Hotel, the site of Sheila's wedding, where they'd rented three rooms— one for Hugo and Meghan, another for Theo, and another for Eva and Finn. The hotel was situated on lush, rolling hills that remained green despite the lateness of the year and lined with a long strip of beach that shimmered like sugar as they drove closer.

"Finn, we have to get married somewhere like this!" Eva shrieked from the back.

Meghan glanced back at her daughter, who held onto one of Finn's hands with both of hers and gazed out at the beach. They weren't yet engaged, but they were well on their way. With a jolt in her gut, Meghan asked herself what that future day might look like. Would she and Hugo still be together? Or would Hugo run off and find this mysterious woman from his past, reminding her of the depths of their longing for one another? Based on what she'd written in the letters, it was clear that the woman would do anything for him.

Hugo pulled the SUV up to the front door of the hotel, where a valet driver accepted the keys, and three bellboys hauled their suitcases and garment bags from the trunk. As they strolled through the front entrance, they spotted several Colemans in the corner, not yet changed into their wedding outfits, chatting in jeans and sweaters, their cheeks pink from the chill and their smiles effervescent.

Samantha Coleman leaped up from the foyer couch to hug them first. She was a beautiful blonde, newly divorced, the daughter of Roland, Meghan and Oriana's long-lost half-brother.

"How was the ferry?" she asked, showering Meghan with her patchouli perfume.

"Freezing," Eva answered, hugging Sam next. "Are your daughters around here?"

"Rachelle and Darcy are with a few of their cousins in the back lounge," Sam explained. "You should join them!"

As Eva, Finn, and Theo headed back, Meghan felt herself drawn into more hugs with Hilary, then Charlie, then her half-brothers, Roland and Grant. Roland looked on the verge of tears, proof that even the most hard-seeming men were softies.

"I've known that little girl since the day she was born," he said to Meghan, speaking of Sheila. "She was always such a sweetheart. It's hard to believe she's grown-up and getting married."

Meghan placed her head gingerly on Roland's shoulder, surprising herself with how at-ease she felt around Roland and Grant. Up until very recently, her brothers hadn't felt up to meeting Oriana and Meghan in person. Their father, Chuck, had abandoned Roland, Grant, and their mother for his second family on Martha's Vineyard, and Roland and Grant had struggled to forgive them. Recently, however, Roland and Grant had stepped in to assist Oriana with her blackmailing debacle, proving themselves to be the protective older brothers Meghan had always secretly hoped they would be.

Even at forty-seven, she'd been able to build more space in her heart for her budding love for them. It was remarkable. A part of her wondered, now, what Roland and Grant would say if she mentioned the letters she'd discovered in the attic. Would they be outraged? Would they demand Hugo explain himself?

"Dad's almost here," Grant explained, interrupting Meghan's reverie.

"Oriana, too," Meghan said. "She had to take the second ferry. Having a toddler in the house doesn't make it easy to get out on time."

"I remember those days," Roland said, eyeing Hilary, Charlie, and Sam knowingly.

Soon afterward, Oriana breezed through the foyer alongside Chuck, whom she'd run into out front. Although Chuck was in his early nineties, he had a bounce to his step, and his eyes were alert, taking everything in. Meghan swallowed her father in a hug, her heart pounding. On her wedding day to Hugo, she and Chuck had danced together for the father-daughter dance, and he'd joked, "If Hugo ever hurts you, I'll kill him!" Meghan had said, "Hugo couldn't hurt a fly."

It was decided that everyone head to their rooms to change, do their makeup and hair, and prepare for the night ahead. Meghan kept herself in-line with Oriana, her arm looped through hers, gabbing about whatever came to her mind as a way to resist Hugo. She dreaded their hotel room, which she now regarded as a prison cell. Since she'd discovered the letters, she'd kept herself sequestered in her study, only coming out long after she knew Hugo was fast asleep. One night, she'd even slept in the guest bedroom and had frequently woken up shivering, moon-light giving the other side of the bed an empty glow.

Oriana's hotel room with Reese was located just down the hall from Meghan and Hugo's. Meghan paused a little too long at Oriana's door, weighing up whether or not she should tell Oriana what was going on in her life. Just as she put her tongue on the roof of her mouth, ready to speak, Reese breezed past her and kissed Oriana lovingly. The sight nearly destroyed her.

And Meghan realized she couldn't tell Oriana what was going on. Oriana's relationship with Reese was gorgeous, honest, and loving. There were no cracks. The idea of revealing her own Grand Canyon-sized crater in her marriage felt debilitating.

"See you after?" Oriana asked with a smile.

"I have a lot of work to do," Meghan tried to joke, gesturing toward her frizzy hair. "Wish me luck."

"You're always gorgeous," Oriana called down the hall as Meghan limped toward her hotel room. There, Hugo waited for her, his key card raised. His eyes swam with curiosity.

"You ready to see the digs?" he asked.

Meghan shrugged, and Hugo scraped the card over the reader and opened the door. Months ago, when they'd reserved the hotel, they'd obsessed over the photographs of the suite, which now appeared before them in real-time: the California King Bed with thousand-count sheets, the jacuzzi near the balcony door, the view of the rolling hills along the beach, the soft light of the November afternoon above the ocean. Although Meghan knew, abstractly, that it was beautiful, the beauty hardly reached her eyes.

"Not bad, huh?" Hugo asked as the door slammed shut behind them.

Meghan closed her eyes, willing herself to live in the moment, to forget about what she'd seen.

"Meghan?"

She opened her eyes to find Hugo removing his sweater to reveal his button-down beneath. How many times had she placed her head on his chest and listened to his heart beating?

"What's going on?" Hugo asked, his eyebrows etched together.

Meghan sighed. "Nothing. I'm just a little out of it."

Hugo stepped closer, wrapped his arm around her waist, and pressed his nose against hers. A wave of hormones flowed through her, brought on by his musk, and Meghan closed her eyes again, wavering between wanting to avoid him and wanting to give into him. Why couldn't she just ask him about the letters? She was frightened of what he'd respond. She was terrified that everything would fall apart immediately.

"What do you say?" Hugo asked softly. "Will you give me a dance later?"

Meghan gazed into his eyes, feeling the heat of his breath on her lips. "If you're good," she said.

Hugo's smile widened mischievously. "My lady, have you ever known me to play by the rules?"

Meghan dressed after that, zipping the forest green dress up her side and eyeing her figure in the mirror. She then added extra makeup, red lipstick, liquid eyeliner, and mascara and curled her hair with her curling iron, loving the way the tight curls flopped to her shoulders. Getting ready for a fancy occasion was always meditative for her, a way of returning back to herself.

Hugo, in a tuxedo, and Meghan took the elevator downstairs and followed in a stream of wedding guests toward the reception hall, where they were given a choice between a "Sheila Cocktail" and a "Jonathon Cocktail." The Sheila Cocktail was vodka-based and bright pink, while the Jonathon Cocktail was founded on whiskey. Meghan opted for Sheila's, while Hugo went for Jonathon's, wrinkling his nose at the strength and the dark smell of it.

"I'm sure Eva and Finn will want to do something like this," Hugo suggested. "Specialty cocktails."

Meghan arched her eyebrow, amazed with herself for giving Hugo the time of day right now. "So, you're excited about their wedding?"

"Of course." Hugo's eyes widened. "I love Finn like a son at this point. And I just want Eva to be happy. If that means a big, swanky wedding with silly cocktails, then so be it."

Had Meghan been happier with Hugo right now, her heart might have shattered at such a kind and loving response. Instead, she drank her Sheila Cocktail too quickly and soon jumped up to have another.

At five-fifteen, the guests of Sheila and Jonathon's wedding were led into the room where the ceremony would be held. Two-hundred and fifty people were in attendance: plenty of Colemans, of course, along with Jonathon's family and multiple characters from across Nantucket and Martha's Vineyard, all of whom wore sleek tuxedos and ornate dresses. Meghan, Hugo, Eva, Finn, and Theo were seated on the bride's side, directly behind Oriana's family, with Meghan on the outer edge that offered the best view of Sheila as she walked down the aisle.

Sheila had many bridesmaids, all of whom wore autumn colors: maroon, dark green, and mustard yellow, and they carried bouquets in celebration of the season. Sheila's maid of honor was her little sister, Marcy, a beautiful young woman who, last summer, had nearly died in a car accident. It had taken her a bit of time to relearn how to walk, but with the help of her boyfriend, Jax, she was off to the races again, strutting down the wedding aisle, making way for her sister.

As Charlie walked Sheila down the aisle, his eyes glinted with tears he wasn't too proud to let fall. Although Meghan had only known Charlie a few months, she saw in his expression her own father's face, and she felt the heaviness of the day— a day of such celebration, of recognizing the passage of time.

Maybe because she forgot herself, Meghan squeezed Hugo's hand during the ceremony. As Sheila and Jonathon pledged to love one another in sickness and in health forevermore, tears sprung to her eyes, and she couldn't help but remember how enthralled she'd been with Hugo when she'd first fallen in love with him. When they'd gotten married after Eva's birth, she'd asked Oriana to pinch her. "I don't know if it's really happening. I can't believe it's real."

The wedding reception was held in the grand hall of the hotel, where a baby grand piano glowed alongside floor-to-ceiling windows, a tremendous chandelier glinted on high, and what looked to be thirty round tables were set up, decorated with white tablecloths and autumnal flowers. Sheila had hired a five-piece string orchestra, violins and cellos and a bass for dinner, but there was talk of a live rock band afterward for dancing. Dinner was steak, and Hugo muttered into Meghan's ear, saying, "This must have cost a fortune. Is that why Charlie was crying going down the aisle?" Meghan allowed a brief laugh to escape her lips before stopping it abruptly.

Eva, Finn, and Theo were seated at the table, as well, slightly buzzed from champagne, eager for the rest of the night to begin. Eva and Finn continued to comment on the wedding to one another, suggesting things they might want to do for theirs. Giggling, Eva said, "Theo, you should be my maid of honor!" To this, Finn said, "No way. He's going to be on my side."

Theo raised his hands diplomatically. "I am happy to fulfill duties on both sides of the aisle."

After Sheila and Jonathon had their first dance as bride and groom, the rest of the guests were invited out on the dance floor to join them. Hugo met Meghan's gaze over the table, looking sheepish. It occurred to Meghan he was frightened of her on-and-off behavior.

"Would the lady like to dance with me?"

Meghan sipped her chardonnay and eyed him nervously. Already, Eva and Finn were out on the dance floor, swaying in time to the ballad. Could Meghan really just fall into Hugo's arms like this? Where was her self-respect?

But she needed more time to think. And she couldn't think properly if Hugo thought there was something really wrong.

"Okay," she breathed, allowing herself to be guided onto the dance floor. There, she slid her fingers through his, touched his shoulder with her opposite hand, and felt the warmth of his upon her lower back. For a moment, she stared off behind his ear, unable to look him in the eye. But soon afterward, the sorrow of that, of missing his gaze, forced her eyes toward his again. His smile opened. Only love was echoed back. But what did it mean?

"You look beautiful tonight," Hugo told her softly.

Meghan's stomach twisted. "You look good, too."

"We should really dance more often," Hugo suggested. "Maybe we should take a class?"

Meghan tried to loosen her fingers from Hugo's, but he held fast.

"Okay, okay," he said, laughing. "We don't have to take a class. I just like dancing with you. That's all."

Meghan's throat was tight, and it was difficult for her to breathe. Blinking away her tears, she continued to sway, willing the song to finish. And when it finally petered out, she heard herself sputter, "I'll be right back. Okay?"

Hugo nodded. "Should I get you another glass of wine?"

"Sure." Meghan fled the dance floor, darting out into the hallway, where she passed a bridesmaid sobbing into her cell phone. These sorts of highly emotional events always brought lonely people to their knees. Instead of entering the bathroom, Meghan bolted toward the wrap-around porch, where she staggered into the crisp cold and took several deep breaths. She hadn't known how close she'd been to fainting until now.

"Meghan?"

Meghan turned to find her father, Chuck, leaning against the railing. The light of the moon illuminated his eyes, and he looked perhaps twenty years younger than his ninety years in the soft night.

"Dad! What are you doing out here?"

Chuck chuckled, adjusting his hands over the railing. "I left during the couple's dance."

Meghan stepped closer to him and placed her hand over one of his. As far as she knew, Chuck had had two great loves in his life, and both of them were now gone.

"I still miss your momma," Chuck offered, his voice breaking. "And I hate standing around in crowds like that, feeling like a silly old man."

"You're not a silly old man," Meghan said, swallowing against the strain in her throat. "And I miss Mom, too. So much."

Chuck tried to smile, but his lips gave up halfway. Inside, the band in the reception hall performed an upbeat tune, but it was muffled through so many panes of glass and hallways, making the music sound as though it was from a different dimension.

"Can I ask you a question?" Meghan asked, surprising herself.

"Anything, honey."

Meghan winced before she said it. "What was it like to be in love with two people at one time?"

Chuck tilted his head thoughtfully. In the reception hall, someone cried out with joy.

"I don't know if I can put words to that," Chuck offered. "But I can try." He scratched his eyebrow and peered out at the water. "I don't condone any of my actions, and you know that. But being in love with my first wife and your mother at the same time was fascinating. I felt as though there were two sides to my heart, my brain, and my life. I was one person with your momma, and I was completely another with my first wife. In a selfish way, I was able to experience so many different facets of my personality, many more than most men are allowed."

Chuck paused as Meghan's head swam with fear.

"Meghan?" Chuck began softly. "Are you thinking about having an affair?"

Meghan's jaw dropped with horror. "Of course not! Oh, I would never." Her heart pounded at the very idea. Although she'd dated a boyfriend in high school, Hugo was the only man she'd ever loved. No other feeling could hold a candle to what she'd always felt for him. Oh, goodness. What was she going to do if this marriage ended? Where would she turn?

Chuck pressed his lips together. "I never thought you would cheat. It was never even a question. I know how much you love Hugo. How much he means to you."

"He means the world," Meghan breathed, her voice breaking.

Chuck's face echoed his curiosity. It was clear he wanted to ask her where this was coming from. But before he could, the porch door opened, and Roland, Grant, and Oriana streamed out, calling their names. For better or for worse, this was the family that had resulted from Chuck's double life. And Meghan chose to live in the joy of what remained, there in the Nantucket moonlight, one island away from where she belonged.

Chapter Four

eghan and Hugo retired to their hotel room at midnight, long before Eva, Finn, and Theo would see their beds. As they'd breezed through the reception hall toward the hallway, they'd spotted Eva, Rachelle, Darcy, and Marcy hovering over nearly full beers, speaking enthusiastically with their hands, and Theo chatting with Jax and Aria, Hilary's daughter. It warmed Meghan's heart that her children had found kindred spirits in the other half of the Coleman family.

Upstairs, Meghan washed her face in the bathroom, watching the dark reds and black inks circle the drain, leaving her pale and tired looking. She changed into silk pajamas and entered the suite, where Hugo lay back in just his boxers and a t-shirt, propping his head up with his elbow as he flicked through the TV stations.

"Good wedding," Hugo said as Meghan sat at the edge of her side of the bed, watching him. "Don't you think?"

Meghan nodded. "Sheila looks happy."

Hugo turned to gaze at her with the same eyes as previously, when they'd danced. She felt his desire for her swanning off of him, and a part of her wanted to give in, to destroy the newfound doubt that poisoned her. But instead, she curled herself over her cell phone, swiping through the photographs she'd taken that evening. Hugo soon returned his attention to the television and eventually drifted off to sleep.

Meghan flicked off most of the lights in the suite, unable to calm herself down. She felt both hot and cold at once, and her thoughts were twisted and garbled as though they were in another language.

The jacuzzi was several feet away from the bed. Based on a test she'd conducted earlier that day, it wasn't loud at all and could be enjoyed, even with Hugo asleep mere feet away. Meghan stepped out of her pajamas and into the jacuzzi, rolling her hair into an up-do that she secured with a hair tie. As the bubbles rolled over her shoulders and the jet streams rammed against her lower back, she tried to think about anything else. But more and more, she burned with curiosity about what she'd seen.

Against her better judgment, Meghan had taken photographs of several of the letters from Hugo's ex-fiancé, which she now pulled up. As though punching herself in the face over and over, she reread some of the most provocative parts, in which Hugo's ex-fiancé declared that she would never love anyone else but him.

We promised each other we would have children by the time we were twenty-three. Don't you remember that? Don't you remember how you said you never wanted anyone else's children but mine?

The letters alternated between anger and arrogance and sorrow, always with a singular message: "I will die without you. Are you really going to do that to me? Are you really going to destroy me like this?"

For Meghan, it begged the question: *What had Hugo written to his ex-fiancé in return? Had he said similar sentences, insinuating that their love was a "once in a lifetime love"?*

This was difficult to imagine, as Meghan had never known Hugo to be sappy. Thinking back to when she'd first met him, she'd thought him to be intelligent, with a whip-smart sense of humor and an ability to tell stories that rivaled some of the greatest novelists. He'd never dipped into immature, romantic language, which had always made their love feel grounded, nourishing, like a warm blanket wrapped around them in the dark.

Meghan had first met Hugo on a balmy summer night. Impossibly, she'd been twenty, and Hugo had been twenty-five. At the time, Meghan was already hard at work on her day trading career, which had required a level of responsibility her friends couldn't quite understand and frequently teased her about. She'd even moved into her own apartment, away from her mother and father, as a way to force herself to grow up even more and not lean too much on her father's wealth. "I'm going to make this career work on my own terms," she'd told him, promising that she'd come over for dinner all the time so as not to break her mother's heart.

Meghan's best friend at the time, Stacy, had dragged her to a beach bonfire, demanding that she "make use of her summer for once in her life. You have to meet someone sometime, you know?" Meghan had been single for several years at that point, having broken up with her high school boyfriend at the age of seventeen. She'd deemed him to be "naive and egotistical" in ways that could have gotten in the way of how driven she was, and so, he'd had to go.

Meghan had worn a miniskirt and a black tank top, her shoulders too exposed beneath the moonlight as the waves crashed to shore before her, and her shoes dug through the wet sand. Around her, other twenty-some-things joked and told stories, engaging with their youth in a way she wasn't fully able to. A part of her blamed Oriana for this. Oriana was focused, charging through New York City with a baby on her hip and an art dealing dream. Meghan didn't want to feel left behind. As always, she wanted Oriana to look at her with respect— and, perhaps, a sense of disbelief for her having done so much on her own. She supposed this was "youngest child" syndrome.

The party was made up of fifty or sixty teenagers and twenty-somethings, islanders who'd been raised in the midst of the most beautiful landscape the United States had to offer, sipping domestic beers, their muscles taut from long days of swimming in the Vineyard Sound. Across the party, beyond some football jocks and a few other people Meghan remembered from high school, was Hugo. He wore a pair of black jeans and a black t-shirt, and his hair was shaggy and curly, his laugh boisterous enough to cut through the barrage of other voices. Meghan had seen Hugo around the island before. He was five years older than her, which meant they hadn't gone to high school together, and in her mind, he had an edge over the other islander guys she knew, if only because he was more-or-less a mystery.

"Isn't there anyone you want to kiss?" Stacy asked girlishly, her eyes shining in the firelight.

"Stacy, we're not thirteen anymore," Meghan scolded

her, her eyes still drawn to Hugo, who was drinking a beer casually, listening intently to something a friend told him. It was rare to meet a man who was actually a good listener, one who wasn't just waiting for his turn to talk.

Stacy giggled. "Don't miss out on your chance, honey. We're only young once, you know?"

Although Meghan had never been a big drinker, she found herself walking through the sand to fetch herself a beer from the big red cooler. She popped the top, feeling awkward, as though she wasn't in full control of her arms.

"Hey, Coleman!" A guy she'd gone to high school with sauntered toward her, flipping his blonde bangs to reveal a sweaty forehead beneath.

Meghan's heart sank. This guy, whose name was on the tip of her tongue, had had a hefty crush on her during Geometry class a few years back, and he hadn't ever gotten the hint to leave her alone. What was it with these kinds of guys? Did they think they ruled the world?

"Oh. Hey."

"How's your summer going?" he asked her, reaching out to clink his beer with hers.

"It's fine?" Meghan's eyes raced across the beach. She felt like a drowning swimmer, reaching out to grab something to hold herself afloat. How could she get away from him?

"That's cool. I think I saw you at the harbor last week. You were eating ice cream with your sister. I couldn't help but notice you."

As Meghan's eyes rolled back into her head, a miracle happened. Out of nowhere, a rogue football whipped through the air and crashed against Meghan's beer. It was thrust out of her hand and flew in a wild parabola over the sands until it smashed to the ground directly in front of

Hugo. As it went, beer gushed across his face, through his perfect hair, and across his t-shirt before it started to douse the sand at his toes.

"Oh my gosh!" Meghan cried, her hand over her mouth.

Around Hugo, everyone cackled, bending forward with glee as Hugo's hair dripped beer. With ease, Hugo stepped forward, raised the beer, and stopped its frothing from the neck with the palm of his hand. He then raised the beer toward Meghan, his eyes connecting with hers across the beach, and Meghan's heart dropped into her stomach. After he cleared the sand from the top, he dropped his head back to drink the beer, his Adam's apple jumping in and out. Everyone cheered. It felt like being in the middle of a beer commercial.

"That was crazy," the guy who'd approached Meghan said, whipping his bangs again.

But Meghan felt drawn toward Hugo, toward this man with such charisma, and she walked away from the kid and toward that handsome, beer-drenched man. When she approached, Hugo's curls continued to drip beer, and she had a strange instinct to reach out and clench them to get the beer out.

"Hi," he said, breaking her silence.

Meghan laughed at herself. She felt as though the air between them was crystallized, easily broken. "I'm so sorry about that."

"Did you do it on purpose?" Hugo asked sneakily.

Meghan's giggles were different than she'd ever heard them, as though being in Hugo's presence transformed her. "No! I mean, no. Of course not." She paused, trying to think of something clever to say. "I mean, I usually don't go around bonfire parties and throw beers at people. Maybe I should start?"

"Sounds dangerous," Hugo suggested.

"I live a life of danger," Meghan uttered, as she thought, *what the heck am I saying?* She'd been possessed. It was the only explanation.

"I don't think I've seen you at one of these parties before," Hugo said. "But you're Meghan, right?"

"And you're Hugo."

"Guilty." Hugo's smile dug a deep dimple into both of his cheeks, and Meghan had the sensation of floating above the sands. About fifteen feet behind Hugo, Stacy popped up with two big thumbs up, cheering her on. As Meghan wrinkled her nose at her, Hugo turned to see what she looked at, which forced Stacy to drop her hands and spin immediately so as not to get caught. Meghan suppressed her laughter.

"I normally avoid these parties," Meghan answered, surprising herself with her honesty. "But it isn't so bad. I like being at the beach at night. The stars look incredible."

Hugo didn't bother to glance up at the sky, and his eyes were large enough to swallow her whole. He sipped the beer that had once been hers and asked, "Can you drive?"

"I'm not drunk at all if that's what you're asking."

Hugo laughed. "You're the only one here."

"Maybe so." Meghan's heart thumped.

"Are you up for doing something spontaneous?" Hugo asked, dropping his chin as though the two of them were in the midst of a conspiracy.

Meghan's initial instinct was to say no, to say goodbye to Hugo, bye to Stacy, and return home so she could wake up bright and early, go for a run, and eat oatmeal. But something in his eyes told her a story she wanted to believe in, and so, she heard herself say, "I'll do anything to get me away from this party."

Hugo downed the rest of the beer in his hand, placed the bottles with the other empties, and waved goodbye to a few of his friends, who looked at Meghan with curiosity and expectation. On the one hand, Meghan didn't like to be seen as just some girl walking away with some guy, but on the other hand, Hugo was arguably the most handsome and charismatic man on that beach, and Meghan was the sort of woman who wanted to win. Although she'd very rarely imagined herself with a romantic partner, as she slid into the driver's seat of her car, Hugo began to float into her vision of her future. How had that happened so quickly? Was she ill?

"Where are we going?" Meghan asked quietly, very aware of Hugo's scent— sand and sea and beer and sweat. Nothing about it rubbed her the wrong way. She'd read in a science book once that humans should mate with humans they liked the sweaty smells of, as it was a sign their genetic makeup was best for procreation. Gosh, what was she thinking?

"I'll guide you," Hugo said conspiratorially, pointing her out of the little makeshift parking lot. "We're headed southwest."

Meghan was nervous, her chest tight, and her words articulate. She barely knew this guy, and she'd allowed him in her car? If her father ever found out about this, he'd freak out.

But the island was small, and the drive to where Hugo wanted to go took no more than fifteen minutes. Finally, he told her to stop her engine at the far end of a long, dirt road, and she sat in the dark silence for a moment, wondering if he'd directed her here to kill her.

"Isn't it amazing?" Hugo's voice was quiet, filled with reverence, as though they were in church.

Meghan followed his line of sight and realized they were parked close to the old Aquinnah Cliffside Overlook Hotel, which had been destroyed in a hurricane back in 1943. There were plenty of rumors about the old place being haunted, that drug people met there to deal and buy, and that people had died there in recent years, messing around on the unsupported top floors. Meghan, being practical, had never entered.

"Let's go," Hugo said, his eyebrows high.

Meghan's chest was tight with panic. "Into the hotel?"

"Where else?"

Hugo popped out of the passenger side, closed the door, and beckoned for Meghan to follow. Meghan was reminded of being a little girl, following Oriana wherever she wanted to go. Unsure of why she did it, she stepped out of her car, closed the door gingerly, and sidled up alongside Hugo. Silently, they moved through the dark, listening as the waves crashed against the cliffs, a reminder of the danger of an ocean neither of them understood.

At the grand entranceway of the once-immaculate hotel, Hugo stalled on the first step and glanced back at Meghan. Meghan's knees knocked together, proof of her fear.

"I've never been inside," Hugo said suddenly. Meghan could see him blush despite the darkness.

Meghan laughed. "You seem like someone who does this all the time."

Hugo stepped back down from the staircase and palmed the back of his neck. "I can't explain it. I wanted to impress you, I guess. Isn't that pathetic?"

Meghan nodded as her heart performed a tap-dance across her diaphragm. "Totally pathetic. I can't respect you anymore."

For a long time, they held the pregnant silence. Meghan had the sudden feeling that she'd always known Hugo, that she'd been born knowing him, that they'd met in previous lives and had always been drawn toward this night. She'd never been romantic in her life, yet here, her heart was on her sleeve.

"Let's just step into the entryway," Meghan breathed, surprising herself. "Let's just see what we can see."

As they entered, Hugo's fingers laced through Meghan's, and Meghan had never felt so brave, so sure. From the foyer, they peered through the inky blackness to make out an enormous ballroom with a ceiling that had been painted immaculately, reminiscent of old Roman cathedrals. It was beyond anything Meghan had ever seen in a book. It was staggering, imagining that anyone had had such artistry, such vision, especially here at the Aquinnah Cliffside Overlook, which had spent the previous fifty years crumbling.

Suddenly, Meghan turned toward Hugo, raised herself up on her tiptoes, and kissed him with her eyes closed— sure of something she'd never imagined she'd be sure of in her life.

They'd spent the rest of the summer like that: in a constant state of being enthralled by one another.

And Meghan had thought they'd spent the previous twenty-seven years like that— completely enamored, lost without one another's touch.

But here in the hotel room in Nantucket Island, hours after Sheila's wedding, forty-seven-year-old Meghan sat alone in the jacuzzi, her eyes closed as she drove through long-lost images of her romantic young adulthood with Hugo. At what point had Hugo met his ex-fiancé? Had he tried to have a second family with her? Had he ever considered Meghan's feelings in any of it?

Perhaps as a way to hurt herself even more, Meghan decided to hunt for Hugo's ex-fiancé on the internet. She only had a first name, but she typed as many possible searches into Google, hunting for her for nearly an hour. As her frustration grew, she became sloppy— and suddenly, during a thirtieth attempt for information, Meghan dropped her phone into the water. Her reflexes took over immediately, and she grabbed the phone from beneath the bubbles and leaped from the jacuzzi. Hugo hardly stirred as she panicked, wrapping her phone in a fluffy white towel. How could she be so stupid? It was three o'clock in the morning, but she had to dress and go to the front desk to ask for a bowl of rice. As she walked through the hallways, not bothering with the elevator, she felt like a ghost in the hotel, so many decades from a version of herself she liked at all.

Maybe Hugo had been right to cheat on her. Maybe she was no good anymore.

Chapter Five

Daniel had hired a twenty-something islander with a love for literature to work at The White Whale Bookstore every Sunday, a necessity as Cindy refused to work that day. Daniel set his alarm early, five-thirty, and did push-ups and sit-ups on the floor of his childhood bedroom, just as he'd done as a teenager when he'd wanted to impress the girls at school. He then padded downstairs and brewed himself a large pot of coffee, which he planned to drink continually throughout the morning as he read. Although he'd always been a big reader, since his wife had announced she was leaving him, he'd fallen deeper into fictional worlds, bent on abandoning his own.

His mother woke up around eight, at which point he helped her change out of her dressing gown and into something warm and practical for sitting around the house. Tenderly, he pulled wool socks along her feet and ankles, glancing up frequently to note the glazed look in her eyes. He then helped her downstairs, cursing himself for still not setting up a bedroom on the ground floor for her. He would do that in the next week or two.

With his mother set up in front of the television, where she liked to be, Daniel made her oatmeal with blueberries and a mug of tea. She could still feed herself, thankfully, although it was often quite messy, requiring a number of paper towels. Although Daniel hated to think of this, it reminded him of when his daughter had been a toddler, throwing food all over herself on her quest to learn how to feed herself. Daniel and Gina had taken many photographs of Caitlin, covered in spaghetti sauce or applesauce or cake and ice cream, delighting in their little lady experiencing the world.

It had been a long time since Daniel had heard from Caitlin. Since Gina had left Martha's Vineyard to return to California, she'd called him twice. When he called, she didn't answer, and Daniel had always imagined her on the other side of the call, sitting in a California sunbeam, sighing with annoyance at her father's neediness.

Around noon, Daniel made his mother some soup and himself a sandwich and sat in front of the television to watch *The Golden Girls*. Frequently, his mother tossed her head back to laugh, and Daniel's heart warmed at this, grateful she could still experience moments of joy, even if she forgot about them a few seconds later.

During a commercial break, his mother glanced over at Daniel and started as though surprised he was there.

"It's a good show," she explained to him, her eyes stirring with confusion. "Lisa showed it to me, you know."

Daniel knew this was not true, that Lisa had never been interested in *The Golden Girls* during her brief time in their home. She would have never spent this kind of quality time with their mother in front of the television.

"Is that right?" he said.

His mother nodded firmly. "She's got a real eye for things, that girl. You could stand to learn a thing or two from her, you know."

Daniel returned his half-eaten sandwich to his plate, his eyes glazing with resentment. Throughout their childhood and teenage years, his mother had made a habit of pitting Daniel and Lisa against one another— frequently citing Daniel's grades as better than Lisa's or Lisa's popularity as stronger than Daniel's. This had created an air of sinister competition in their home, one that hadn't allowed Daniel and Lisa to ever see eye to eye. When Daniel had gotten stood up before prom, Lisa had howled with laughter— calling out to their mother, "I guess Danny can do the dishes tonight after all, Ma!"

"Did you hear what I said?" his mother demanded, her eyes icy. Again, she looked precisely as she had twenty-five years ago, far before the diagnosis, when it had seemed that her evil streak had been what kept her alive and strong.

"Don't let your soup get cold, Mom," Daniel reminded her quietly, knowing it wasn't in his best interests to argue with her. It would just confuse her.

As Daniel washed the dishes after lunch, *The Golden Girls'* laugh track echoed in the living room. His fingers thick with suds, he imagined, not for the first time, what it would be like to put his mother in a nursing home. That way, he could close down the bookstore, cut his losses, and move somewhere far away. He could forget about Gina, about the daughter who hated him, about his cruel mother, and about his sister, who'd abandoned him. He could become someone else.

Maybe, if he was far away, he could find a way to forgive all of them and start anew.

But no. He cut the water, his head swimming with sorrow. There was no way he could bring himself to drop their mother off at a nursing home, no way he could live with himself. He genuinely believed children were meant to care for parents as they aged, the way parents had cared for their children. It was the nature of things, one of life's unavoidable cycles.

If only Lisa was here. If only she would help him carry half of the weight of their mother's illness. Yes, their mother had always been horrible to them. But she was just a little old woman now. She needed them.

Daniel leaned against the entryway between the living room and kitchen, watching the blue light from the television play against his mother's thin skin. When the commercial broke, he couldn't help himself but say, "I do love you, Mom."

At this, his mother bucked around, frightened by the sound of his voice. It was a sentence that hadn't been said often in that house, certainly a sentiment that didn't belong.

Instead of answering him, his mother asked, "Is Lisa on her way home? I'm making pork chops," and returned her attention to the screen, where *The Golden Girls* would never abandon her.

Chapter Six

The morning after Sheila's wedding, Sam hosted a Coleman brunch. Rachelle, the chef of the family, helmed the work in the kitchen, crafting Eggs Benedict, bacon, avocado toast, fresh scones, and scrumptious cakes with mandarin and lemon. Meghan hovered in the kitchen, having asked several times if there was anything she could do to help and been told "no" enough times. She sipped a mimosa as Sam and Hilary alternated between squabbling and laughing, and Darcy and Rachelle jumped from the stovetop to the counter to the oven, keeping tabs on everything. Oriana was next to Meghan, easily entering the conversation as she pleased. Meghan felt as though she had three heads, as though she didn't belong and never had. She hadn't spoken in maybe twenty minutes. Eventually, she went to the bathroom and stared at herself in the mirror, demanding herself to pull it together. But after the phone incident very early this morning and her panic surrounding her marriage, she felt as though she'd come from another planet.

Samantha, Hilary, and their mother, Estelle, set the

dining room table, and Samantha's boyfriend, Derek, set up a speaker system to play light jazz music. Oriana refilled Meghan's mimosa glass and complimented Meghan's light pink sweater, which Meghan had forgotten she was wearing.

"You look so much better in pink than I do," Oriana said with a sigh. "I'm jealous."

Meghan wasn't sure how to take this compliment. She sipped her mimosa and tried to pull her lips into a smile. Before she could respond, Sam appeared and began to chat to Oriana about her daughter, Alexa, who was on her way to The Jessabelle House, having taken Benny to a playground beforehand.

"That little kid wears us out," Oriana said of her grandson.

Sam lowered her voice, glancing back toward the kitchen. "I cannot wait to be a grandmother. I'm jealous."

Oriana beamed. "Your time will come. I keep telling that to Meg, too."

Just as soon as Alexa appeared with Benny on her hip, Sam announced it was time to sit down for brunch. "Everyone's here! I hope you're hungry!" Meghan walked like a zombie toward the table, collapsing in the chair beside Oriana, avoiding eye contact with Hugo, who sat across from her. She felt herself using Oriana as protection, as though, as long as her older sister was there, she could hide from the darkness that lurked on the other side of this weekend.

"Let's all raise a glass to toast the beautiful Sheila and the newest member of the Coleman family, Jonathon!" Chuck announced, beaming across the long table toward his granddaughter.

Sheila's eyes glinted with tears as she held Jonathon's

hand over the table. They looked exhausted, as though they'd been awake all night celebrating with friends, but their skin was peachy and bright, proof of their youth and vitality. Meghan raised her glass and heard herself congratulate the young couple again.

Throughout the meal, Meghan spoke infrequently. She felt as though she bathed in other people's conversations, allowing their words to wash over her. Once or twice, Hugo referenced something Meghan and Hugo had done together— a restaurant they'd tried or a hike they'd done, and Meghan felt herself nod in confirmation. Yes, they'd done that together, back when she'd been sure about them. Back when they'd been on solid ground.

After brunch, Meghan retreated to the guest bedroom, where she'd left her phone in a bag of rice. She raised the bag into the light and stared at the dark brick, wondering if it was too early to start it back up again. The internet had said twenty-four hours was best.

Besides, who did she want to call? Everyone she loved in the world was at The Jessabelle House. And she wasn't sure she could tell any of them what was on her mind.

To clear her head, Meghan donned her winter coat, her hat, and her mittens and retreated to the terrace, where a sharp wind bit her cheeks and whipped her hair out behind her. The long stretch of beach beckoned, and her muscles itched to move, to draw her away from the warm claustrophobia of that party. She bucked down the staircase and shot toward the beach, drawn toward the glowing waves that surged toward her. Just before she reached the water, she heard a voice behind her calling out, "Mom! Wait up!"

Meghan froze, her hands shoved deep in her pockets.

Eva's breath was ragged behind her, followed by another's. She wasn't alone.

"Why did you sneak out like that?" Theo laughed, teasing her as he buttoned his coat to his chin.

Eva laced her arm through her mother's and dropped her head against her shoulder. "I ate too much. I needed a walk, too."

Surrounded by her children, Meghan breathed easier. Still unable to speak, she walked along the water, her shoes shifting in the sand.

"Are you having an okay time?" Eva asked, her voice higher pitched than normal. She sensed something was up.

"The food was insane," Theo said, filling the silence.

"Yes. Rachelle is very talented," Meghan said softly.

Eva stalled, narrowing her eyes. "Mom. What is going on?"

Meghan arched her eyebrow. "Nothing?"

Theo dragged his toe through the sand. After a long pause, he coughed and said, "We're worried about you though?"

"I saw the bag of rice," Eva confessed.

"I just dropped my phone in the stupid jacuzzi," Meghan explained.

"Oh. That happens." Eva nodded, clearly hoping that was the single reason for her mother's terrible mood.

Meghan traced her teeth with her tongue, imagining what would happen if she came out with the truth. Eva and Theo were intelligent children, in-tune with their parents' dynamic. They were the only people in the world who knew Hugo half as well as Meghan did (at least, she'd thought this before finding the letters). Maybe they were the only people in the world who could tell Meghan what to do.

"I found something in the attic," Meghan began, her words syncopated and breaking at the edges. "Something that might have changed my entire life. And I don't know what to do."

Eva frowned. "What do you mean? What did you find?"

Meghan hated the fact that admitting she'd found the letters made them even more real.

"They were letters from a woman who loved your father very much," Meghan continued, her cheeks flashing with heat from the tremendous embarrassment. "And it's clear that he loved her, too. They were engaged; they were planning a future. But something happened, something that she doesn't write about in the letters." Meghan closed her eyes against her tears, willing herself to be stronger. "I don't know when the letters were written. They're not dated. And I can't help but think that your father had some kind of affair, that he was plotting to leave us and start a new family with her."

Meghan's voice was shaky, proof of her terror. Eva and Theo stared at one another, Eva with her lips parted and Theo ripping his fingers through his long hair.

"And even if the letters are from before we got together," Meghan continued, realizing this was her chance to get everything out in the open, "they make me question everything. Your father never ever mentioned her. Not in all our years together. It makes me wonder how much I actually know him. He was supposed to be my life partner. He was supposed to be my everything."

Eva's eyes filled with tears, and Meghan hurried to

apologize, to admit she'd gone too far. But before she could, Eva stuttered, "Theo, oh my God."

Theo was very pale, his eyes flickering back and forth as though he couldn't look at Meghan. This wasn't the reaction Meghan had expected. A large part of her, she realized, had assumed her children would calm her worries, that they would tell her their father could only love one woman, and that was her.

"We found them," Eva whispered, her voice rasping, as Theo nodded ponderously.

Meghan's knees dropped beneath her, nearly casting her to the sand. The wind howled in her ears.

"What are you saying?" Meghan demanded harshly, taking a step away from them.

Eva sniffed and stared at Theo as though demanding he take the reins.

"I mean, it was kind of crazy," Theo stuttered. "We were looking for a place to hide vodka we'd bought?"

"Like a million years ago," Eva said.

"We were in the attic," Theo went on. "And we stumbled onto the box. The one with the ribbon on it."

"We shouldn't have even opened it," Eva whispered. "I don't even remember why we did."

"Curiosity? Stupidity?" Theo hurried to add.

Meghan's heart thrummed in her chest. "You read all of them?"

"I hated them, Mom," Eva said, her voice very tight. "I hate that woman. I hate everything about her."

Meghan took another step backward, her shoulders quivering in the chill. "How old were you?"

Theo set his jaw and looked to his older sister for an answer, as though anything they said could get them out of this mess. Meghan recognized the fear in Eva's eyes, proof she knew they'd messed up.

"I told you we should have thrown them away," Eva rasped to Theo as though Meghan wasn't there.

Theo tugged at his hair again so that his forehead was white as snow. "I didn't want to just throw away Dad's memories! He'd kept them for a reason!"

Meghan's thoughts were suddenly clear, a result of the horror of this moment. "Let me get this straight," she said, her tone hard and sure. "You were teenagers when you found these letters?"

Eva swallowed, her cheeks pale. "I was eighteen, maybe."

"So, Theo, you were sixteen," Meghan recited, stating facts. "Which means you knew about your father's ex-fiancé for the past eight years, and you didn't think to tell me?"

Eva slumped forward, cradling her elbows with her hands. Theo looked just as he had as a little kid, too frightened to go down the slide. Meghan had always had to coax him. *Come on, Theo. You can do it!*

Eva jumped in the sand, the emotion of this moment making her fidgety and strange. "We didn't want it to get into your head," she rasped, forcing her eyes toward Meghan's. "We didn't want you to think Dad didn't love you!"

"He loves you so much, Mom," Theo blared. "I've watched so many of my friends' parents get divorced. They're not like you guys."

"We were too young to understand, Mom," Eva tried.

"You were eighteen, Eva," Meghan pointed out flatly. "You were old enough for almost everything else. Why not this?"

With her children speechless, stuttering through the weight of this moment, Meghan turned to peer out across the thrashing waves. She felt as though she was out there, giving in to them, being tossed around until she drowned. When she'd met Hugo, she'd felt the warmth of his love wrap around her, becoming the stability she hadn't known she'd craved.

"Mom! Say something," Eva begged. She wanted Meghan to tell her it was all right, that she understood why her children had lied. She wanted her mother to bandage it all up to make it okay. But Meghan was beyond that right now.

"You knew it was strange he never mentioned it," Meghan said finally. "You knew there was something off."

Eva had begun to cry, tears shivering down her cheeks, which were blotched red from chill and sorrow.

"We love you guys," Theo blubbered softly.

"You obviously don't love me enough to show me this respect," Meghan said firmly. "You've proven that to me."

Meghan turned on her heel and walked the opposite direction down the beach, daring her children to chase after her, to say one thing that would redeem them in her eyes. But she knew there was nothing that they could offer, no words to mend her heart. Far up on the bluffs, she could make out the laughter echoing from The Jessabelle House, a place she knew she would have to return to to keep up the lie.

Chapter Seven

Daniel's best friend from high school was Craig Middleton, and in the two years since Daniel had returned to care for his mother, he and Craig had rekindled their friendship. Craig had never left the island, boasted that he'd hardly gone on vacation over the years because "who needs anything else but this?" and was a remarkable six foot six inches, which made him a little too tall to be deemed "handsome." Daniel's five feet and eleven inches were minuscule in comparison.

Craig came over Tuesday night after Daniel's hard twelve-hour day at the bookstore. He carried a six-pack of beer in his left hand and waved through the front window as he approached, reminding Daniel of the hundreds of times Craig had walked up that driveway during high school, ready to drag Daniel to a night of board games or even to the library, a place they'd adored. They hadn't been invited to many parties, not like Lisa. Although Craig had admitted, back then, that Lisa was attractive, he'd been too frightened of her to ever speak to her. She'd always had a boyfriend, anyway— a popular guy who'd hardly glanced Daniel's way when they were at school.

"Hey, man!" Craig was boisterous as he entered, placing the six-pack of beer on the counter and rubbing his palms together. "How's the day?"

"Living the dream," Daniel joked, taking a beer and popping the top. Just fifteen minutes earlier, he'd helped his mother to bed, which had graciously gone easier than normal. The beer was cold and malty against his tongue, and he was momentarily grateful that he and Craig no longer had to drink the cheapest beer available.

Craig and Daniel sat in the living room in front of the sports channel, which they put on silent so they could talk.

"I don't know, man," Craig was saying, "I've begun to think of my divorce as the greatest thing that ever happened to me. Amy and I were sleepwalking for so much of our lives, you know? We got married because we wanted to get pregnant, and then, a baby never came, and we just slowly turned away from each other. That doesn't mean I don't have the utmost respect for her. I mean, the social media empire she's built is incredible."

Daniel nodded, having perused Craig's ex's social media channels, wherein she posted instructional videos for crafts around the house: making bath bombs or bird feeders or lamps out of random material. Amy was good-looking and garrulous, and, in the wake of her divorce from Craig, she'd started dating one of the teachers at the high school, which Daniel was pretty sure got on Craig's nerves. He didn't go on about it, though. He'd decided to be positive about everything, which was both inspiring and annoying at once.

"I have another date this week," Craig continued,

removing his phone to bring up a dating app. "She's an artist. Look at her paintings!"

Daniel took the phone and flicked through the photographs, which revealed Craig's date to be a forty-something woman with a love for painting scenes of fields and horses. Although they weren't Daniel's thing, he recognized her talent— and her beauty. His heart shifted with something like jealousy.

"Man, I'm telling you," Craig went on. "You should just go out with one woman, just to see what's out there." He paused, seeming to weigh up if he wanted to say it, before adding, "I know you're still struggling to sign the papers. But maybe just seeing yourself back out in the dating scene will help."

Daniel took a long swig of beer, feeling a sense of Deja Vu. How many times had Craig and Daniel discussed girls back in their teenage years, with Craig analyzing them as though they were mathematical equations he could solve? Daniel hadn't met Gina until he'd moved out to California, a time that had triggered in him a sense of self-confidence that had probably fooled Gina into thinking he was someone he wasn't.

"Just download the app," Craig urged. "Let's see who you match with."

Sensing he couldn't get out of this, not with Craig halfway done with only his first beer, Daniel begrudgingly downloaded the app and uploaded three photographs of himself (all of which Gina had taken approximately two years ago, before the separation). When the app asked him to write a "bio," he blinked dumbly at Craig. "How am I supposed to describe myself in one hundred and forty characters?"

Craig cackled. "You're a book guy, Daniel. You should be able to come up with something."

Daniel sighed and typed: "A book guy. Non-readers need not swipe."

He showed the bio to Craig, who cackled. "Sassy. I like it."

"Will women like it?" Daniel asked, wincing at how stupid he sounded.

"Lots of women read on this island," Craig pointed out. "I always see them on their e-readers on the beach."

Daniel wanted to point out that e-reader women weren't his target— that he owned a bookstore because he loved the intimacy of reading a real book, turning the pages. Still, he couldn't be picky. He published his profile, which allowed him to begin swiping on women in his immediate area— between the ages of forty and sixty. Craig hovered behind him, sipping his beer and commenting.

"I think I saw her at the grocery store today," he said of a woman with silver hair and a soft smile. Next: "Oh, she's beautiful, Daniel. You're crazy if you don't swipe right."

Each time another face appeared on Daniel's screen, his stomach tightened into knots, and he struggled to make sense of what he was doing. Gina had been his whole world. It was nearly impossible to imagine himself out to dinner with someone who wasn't her.

"She says she likes books!" Craig cried out, pointing at the newest face on the screen— a forty-nine-year-old woman named Victoria with bottle-red hair and several photographs of her laughing with girlfriends. In her bio, she'd written: "I'm loving life, reading the afternoons away, and would prefer to be out on a sailboat than just about anywhere else on earth. Swipe if you're up for an adventure. :)"

"She sounds great, Daniel," Craig insisted. "Seriously! If you don't swipe, you're insane."

Daniel's thumb shivered as he shot the photograph to the right of his screen. Miraculously, a green sign filled the screen, along with the words: **YOU HAVE A MATCH!** Daniel's eyes bugged out of his head as Craig walloped with laughter.

"She likes you, too! You can run off and read on a sailboat together!" Craig clapped his shoulder and shook him.

Daniel sat, dumbfounded for a moment. He hated to admit how pleased he was, as though this single moment of validation had eliminated his day's sorrows.

"You have to write to her!" Craig explained. "Ask her out this week!"

Daniel scrunched up his nose. "I don't know. I mean, someone has to be here with Mom."

"Can't you ask your nurse to stay late?" Craig suggested. "Come on, man. Push yourself."

Daniel sighed and began to type, second-guessing every sentence as though this was the first time he'd ever corresponded with a woman. Lucky for him, with Craig's insight and coaching, by the time he finished his beer, he had a date lined up with Victoria Thursday night. Craig did a victory dance in the center of the room, cracked two more beers for them, and announced this was the next phase of the rest of Daniel's life. "Man, just you wait. You're fifty now. Remember how nervous we were around girls as teenagers? Those nerves don't exist anymore. You'll be confident and sure of yourself, and Victoria won't be able to resist you."

* * *

On Thursday night, Daniel sat alone in a swanky Oak Bluffs wine bar, wearing a navy blue button-down and a pair of his nicer jeans, studying the painting of a light-house on the far wall and willing himself to disappear into the scene. Victoria was three minutes late, and nerves were like needles across his neck and chest, making it difficult for him to breathe. He made a mental note to tell Craig just how wrong he'd been about being "so much more confident" in the dating department at the age of fifty. He hadn't dated as a teenager— but when he'd begun, at least he'd had a completely-full head of hair, a six-pack, and a smooth forehead. He couldn't say the same for himself now.

The bar was mostly full, and Daniel recognized several islanders from their perusals in his bookshop, including one older woman who frequently came in asking for cozy mysteries. Daniel had stocked the book-store with cozy mysteries just for her, in fact, and as he glanced her way a second time that night, she raised her hand and waved excitedly, saying something to her husband that made him turn and salute Daniel. Daniel imagined her saying, "That's that sad bookstore owner I was telling you about!"

But before Daniel could get bogged down in his imag-ination, Victoria appeared in the doorway. She wore a maroon dress with a turtleneck, black tights, and black boots, and she was prettier than she'd been in her photographs, which Craig had told him was not typical.

"Daniel?" Victoria stopped in front of his table and gave him a nervous smile.

"Victoria! Hi." Daniel stood and extended his hand to

shake hers, which seemed oddly formal. Should he have hugged her? He didn't even know her!

"Sorry I'm a little bit late," Victoria said as she slid onto the chair across from him. "I couldn't find a parking spot. Crazy, this late in the year, huh?"

"Feels like everyone came out tonight," Daniel said, cursing himself for not saying something more interesting. He forced his mouth shut, stifling his next boring question about what kind of car she drove. Oh, God. He was not good at this.

The waiter arrived to take their orders, saving Daniel's life, and Victoria asked him four questions about the wine list before opting for chardonnay. Daniel ordered a Primitivo and a bowl of olives, remembering that Gina had adored olives; they'd always gotten them at wine bars back in California. But as the waiter retreated, Victoria wrinkled her nose and said, "Ugh. I hate olives."

"Oh! I'm so sorry." Daniel was suddenly floored with another influx of nerves.

"Don't worry." Victoria giggled and adjusted her weight on her chair. "So. You're a book guy?"

"I wasn't sure what to write on the bio," Daniel explained timidly. "But I own a bookstore here in Oak Bluffs."

Victoria brightened. "The Dog-Eared Corner?"

"No. That's in Edgartown. I'm a few streets away. The White Whale?"

Victoria waved her hand. "I think I walked past it, maybe. My friend told me you don't have that many thrillers?"

"Thrillers are your game?"

"I'm obsessed with them." Victoria opened both of her hands like clams and stared at the ceiling. "I don't know what it is about the scary things that happen to people, but I love reading about them. You know?"

Daniel felt he'd had enough scary things in his life so far; he wasn't so keen on reading thrillers as they elevated his anxiety. But instead of explaining, he said, "People love thrillers. I really should order more for the bookstore."

"Wow! My very own book dealer," Victoria said. "Of course, I mostly read on my e-reader. It's just easier, you know?"

The waiter returned with their wine and Daniel's olives, and Daniel took two large gulps before he realized Victoria wanted to clink her glass with his. Gosh, he was rude. Then again, he had no idea what to say to her love of e-readers, so he remained silent, raised his glass, and tried to smile as Victoria said, "This is my fourth date this week. But I usually don't go out with islanders."

Daniel felt as though he was having heart palpitations. "This is your fourth date this week?"

Victoria rolled her shoulders back. "I'm looking for a guy with a sailboat. My most recent ex had one, and I just loved going out on it."

"Well, I don't know what to tell you. I don't have a sailboat. I just have a bookstore." That, and an ailing mother, a wife he still hadn't divorced, and a daughter who wouldn't talk to him.

Victoria raised her lips. "Do you have any interest in sailing?"

"I was raised here on the island, so I know how," Daniel explained. "My friend Craig's dad taught us when we were teenagers. I've barely gone since I moved back to the island, though. The bookstore takes up so much of my time."

Victoria's eyes were glazed with disinterest. "Oh? When did you come back?" She sounded bored out of her mind.

"Two years ago," Daniel explained. "My mom got sick, and I convinced my wife to move out here so I could open a bookstore and take care of her. But, as you can see, that didn't work out." He gestured toward the table, toward their date in general, to which Victoria swallowed one-half of her glass of wine and wrinkled her nose.

Obviously, she was allowed to talk about her search for a guy with a sailboat, and he wasn't allowed to talk about his broken heart. Whatever.

After a very long silence, Daniel forced himself to ask her, "Where did you grow up?" To this, Victoria launched into a narrative about her birth in Maine, her mother's acting career, her father's auto shop, and her continual quest for money. She was more-or-less happy these days after her most recent divorce from a very rich man who'd died shortly after they'd parted ways. Daniel felt as though he was listening to the worst radio show on earth. Frequently, he stared at the exit, willing time to move faster. And when the waiter arrived to ask if they wanted another drink, Daniel nearly yelled, "Actually, can we just get the check?"

Victoria wasn't used to being rejected. Immediately, her face turned a pickled green, and she shot up from the table, raised her chin, and said, "Your bookstore sucks, by the way. And you need to lose weight." She then turned on her heel and walked out of the wine bar.

Daniel had never been more relieved in his life. He also thought he might be having a panic attack. His mouth was very dry, a result of the wine, and he dropped his face into his hands as his shoulders shook. For a long time, he remained like that, feeling as though the rest of the world would just go on without him; he wasn't a necessity in anyone's story, save for his mother, who couldn't remember him.

Breaking through his reverie, someone set something down with a dull clunk on his table. He raised his head to find a large glass of water in front of him, filled with delicious ice, and he traced his eyes leftward to find a woman in her late forties beside him, smiling with a mix of worry and curiosity. She had brown hair with attractive blonde highlights, cat-eyeglasses, and bright red lipstick, and she was lean with a good posture, suggesting she did Pilates or yoga. For a moment, she held his gaze and then said, "You need to drink that water. Please."

Daniel wasn't accustomed to being looked after. Unsure what to do, he drank from the glass she'd brought him, feeling his thoughts slow and his heart stop pumping so quickly. As he drank, the woman sat on the edge of the chair across from him, making sure he finished.

"Thank you," he managed afterward.

The woman raised her shoulders. "I was sitting at that table over there," she pointed behind her, "and heard what Victoria said to you. Gosh, she's a vile woman, isn't she?"

Daniel couldn't help but roll with laughter. It felt delicious to laugh but unfamiliar, and he stopped soon afterward as it was too surprising. "How do you know her?"

"I met her at a volunteer event last summer," she explained. "She was hitting on everyone in sight, trying to find a rich boyfriend. Was it an internet date?"

Daniel nodded. "I'm embarrassed to admit that."

"Why? Everyone dates online these days."

"Do you?"

The woman raised her left hand and turned it to show her engagement and wedding rings. "I got married a very long time ago. The idea of getting back out there terrifies me. You're a brave soul."

The waiter returned with the check for Daniel, but the woman addressed him instead, asking for another rosé. "I was sitting over there," she explained. "But I'd like to move. If I'm not bothering you too much?"

"Not at all. I'll have another Primitivo," he said to the waiter. "Thanks."

"I'm Meghan, by the way," the woman said, reaching over to shake Daniel's hand. "I heard you say you own The White Whale Bookstore?"

"Did you listen to our entire conversation?" Daniel teased.

"To be honest, I was looking for a distraction," Meghan explained.

"That's part of the reason for places like these, I guess," Daniel said. "I'm Daniel, by the way. The fool of the night."

"And I'm the fool of the decade," Meghan announced.

Daniel laughed, surprised, sensing the self-hatred and resignation behind the words. "You don't look like a fool."

Meghan blew up her bangs and rolled her eyes the way a child might have. "I can't remember you, Daniel. From growing up here." She winked. "I overheard that, too."

Daniel laughed. "How old are you?"

"Forty-seven. And you?"

"Fifty," Daniel explained.

"And you went to Oak Bluffs High?"

"Guilty," Daniel said. "But I kept a low profile. I was really into reading and board games."

"I wasn't exactly keen on the high school parties, either," Meghan said. "We must have missed each other, like two ships passing in the night."

"I wouldn't have known how to talk to women back then," Daniel explained. "Not even on a friend level."

Meghan tilted her head.

Before she could respond, Daniel added, "Maybe you heard I was married? I got a little bit better at it. Well, I thought I had. When she left me here in Martha's Vineyard, all my game went out the window, I'm afraid."

Meghan sighed. "I cannot imagine anyone leaving Martha's Vineyard on purpose."

"She was a California girl. I couldn't get her to appreciate the Atlantic Ocean."

"What's so great about the Pacific?" Meghan joked.

"I've been asking myself the same thing." Daniel laughed, remembering how he'd adored the Pacific, how he'd carried his daughter along the beach and watched grand sunsets like orange and pink explosions, swallowing the entire sky.

"It wasn't just Martha's Vineyard that broke us up," Daniel admitted finally.

"It's never just one thing, is it?"

Daniel raised his shoulders, noting he'd already drunk through his second glass of wine. The waiter eyed them like a hungry shark, ready to elevate his tip. Meghan waved him over, suggesting they order another round. Daniel jumped at the chance, genuinely surprised at the comfort he felt in Meghan's presence, how easily his lungs filled with oxygen, how readily he said every joke. He felt more like the man he'd been when Gina had fallen in love with him— a version of himself he'd respected.

As the night wore on, the world around their table blurred, and Daniel found himself falling deeper into the sound of Meghan's voice. A part of him wondered: *where had she been all his life?* And another screamed: *be careful! She's married.* But at no time was Daniel necessarily attracted to Meghan, although she was beautiful. Instead, he found in her a worthy conversationalist, one who put people like Victoria to shame.

Toward the end of the night, as Meghan pulled out her credit card and insisted on paying for them, she raised her opposite finger and said, "I cannot tell you how much I needed a friend tonight." The honesty in her eyes nearly shattered Daniel's heart.

"I've needed a friend for ages," Daniel breathed, wondering what Meghan meant. Perhaps her husband was cruel to her. Perhaps he ignored her. Perhaps she was on the brink of a divorce, too. But he didn't want to pry.

"Then let's do this again!" Meghan threw up her arms exuberantly.

Embarrassingly, Daniel felt like a little kid who'd been invited to someone's birthday party. For the first time in ages, he felt included in life, in what normal people did with their day-to-day.

"Let's do it," Daniel said, and then, before he chickened out, he asked, "Can I get your phone number?"

Meghan winced. "I'm between phones at the moment. Long story. Can I call you at the bookstore when I get another one?"

Daniel laughed. "Hardly anyone calls that phone, but I always answer it."

Chapter Eight

Meghan sat in her study Saturday morning, her laptop opened as she studied the graphs she'd built for herself, analyzing what she'd bought and sold thus far this month. Outside the window, robust snow fluttered from clouds thick as a milkshake, and down the hall, Hugo was doing something aerobic, causing the floorboards to shriek beneath him. He'd announced to her that morning that the roads were too icy to run on, and she'd shrugged and said, "There's a jump rope in the garage," and taken her coffee upstairs.

Meghan had been icy with Hugo since Sunday, to say the least. But more than that, she'd completely ignored her children, demanding that Hugo take the lead on showing Theo the ropes of day trading and barely skimming Eva's text messages. Thursday evening, after Meghan had returned home from her glorious time at the wine bar, Hugo had been seated in the living room with a glass of whiskey, his eyes damaged. It was written all over his face that he knew there was something wrong; he also knew she didn't want to talk about it. Meghan had a hunch her children were unwilling to bring up the letters to their father themselves.

Every day in that house felt like living next to a bomb ticking toward an explosion.

Suddenly, there was a knock at Meghan's study door. This was curious, as Hugo's squeaking hadn't ceased; he was still in the midst of whatever cardio he'd decided upon.

"Hello?" Meghan tilted her head.

"Mom?" It was, of course, Eva there to patch things up. "Can I come in?"

Meghan sighed, stood from her desk, and walked toward the door. When she opened it, she found her daughter stricken, her cheeks slack, and her clothing messy— a pair of sweatpants, a sweatshirt that didn't match, plus a t-shirt with a stain on it. This wasn't the daughter Meghan had raised.

"Can I come in?" Eva asked quietly.

Meghan glanced back at her computer graphs. "I'm in the middle of something."

"It won't take long," Eva said. "Please."

Meghan stepped back to allow Eva inside, then closed the door behind her and gestured toward the ochre couch. Eva sat and crossed her ankles, then pulled her legs up onto the cushion. Her socks had holes in them.

"I know you're ignoring me," Eva stammered. "And I don't know what to do."

Meghan sat in her swivel computer chair and continued to gaze out the window. Abstractly, she remembered that she still hadn't put up any of the Thanksgiving decorations but that nobody had thought to comment on it. Probably, nobody had ever appreciated her decorating efforts. What had she been doing all these years?

"I don't know what to do, either," Meghan told her daughter coldly.

Eva sniffed, on the verge of tears. Meghan glanced back at her daughter, her heart melting the tiniest bit.

"We were so young and stupid when we found them, Mom," Eva hurried to tell her. "We totally freaked out. I cried for days, and Theo was a mess, too."

Meghan's eyebrows rose. "Must have been terrible." She wasn't convinced.

Eva nodded firmly, her ponytail jumping around behind her. "I know we should have told you. I understand that now."

"Do you really understand?" Meghan breathed, her heart racing. "How would you feel if all the people you loved the most in the world were keeping a secret from you?" Meghan leaned over in her chair so that her eyes were only a foot or so from Eva's. She felt fiery and on the edge of losing everything, which made her dangerous to be around.

Eva stuttered. "I would feel terrible." She closed her eyes. "But what if it's a misunderstanding?"

"It's not," Meghan told her. "There are lies all around me, and I'm struggling to hold myself together."

Eva's eyes welled with tears. "Is there anything I can do to fix this?"

"I need time, Eva," Meghan blared as, down the hall, the floorboards continued to creak, signaling another round of Hugo's cardio.

In a very small voice, Eva said, "You can't box us out forever. Thanksgiving is coming, and..." She rubbed her temples as though trying to force herself to think of another tactic.

"Maybe we won't do Thanksgiving this year," Meghan said calmly. "Maybe we'll skip Christmas, too."

Eva's jaw dropped. For a long time, she stared at Meghan as though she'd never seen her before, then stood up, adjusting her sweatshirt over her shoulders.

"You should wash that t-shirt, honey," Meghan said as she left her study. "It's not a good look."

Immediately after the study door clicked closed behind Eva, Meghan melted into her hands, her shoulders shaking. Never in her life had she treated Eva like this! Never in her life had she felt so cruel! But her heart was slashed to pieces, and she felt as though she free-fell through the sky with no sense of gravity.

And then, she remembered something.

Meghan laced her shoes, whirled her winter coat over her shoulders, and hurried out the front door without telling Hugo her plans. Feeling like a teenager breaking out of the house, she started the engine and drove very slowly down the icy, snowy road. The drive to downtown Oak Bluffs was no more than ten minutes, usually, but in these conditions, it took her closer to twenty.

The parking spaces in front of the pale blue Victorian were wide open, presumably because so many had decided to stay home due to the weather. Meghan shut off the engine and walked gingerly up the sidewalk, praying he was in. Although she'd promised to call when her new cell came in, it still hadn't, and she enjoyed the feeling of being rootless, uncontactable.

Daniel was seated behind the counter, doing what every bookstore owner was meant to be doing: he was reading. As the bell jangled above the door, he bucked up, surprised, then produced the brightest smile Meghan had seen in ages. It had been a long time since she'd made someone so happy just by showing up.

"Meghan!" Daniel snuck a bookmark between his pages and walked around the counter. "This is a surprise."

"It's a surprise for me, too," Meghan told him. "But I realized, funnily enough, that I don't have a book to read right now. Terrible, isn't it?"

Daniel laughed. "That might be the worst feeling in the world. And I don't say that lightly. What kind of stuff do you like to read?"

"Maybe you can guide me?" Meghan suggested, eyeing the long lines of shelves filled with books in all colors of the rainbow. "I heard a rumor you're not into thrillers, though. So, nothing like that."

"There are some fantastic thrillers," Daniel assured her. "But I have a feeling you want something a little more emotional. Maybe women's fiction?"

Meghan's nose quivered. "That might be a little too close to home right now."

"I see. You're looking for escapism?"

"I think so," Meghan said.

"Romance?"

"No!" Meghan chuckled at her own outburst and tucked her hair behind her ears. "I mean, no. Nothing to do with love."

Daniel scoured the bookshelves, his brow furrowed, seeming to try his best to integrate his limited knowledge of Meghan with his wide under-standing of literature. Eventually, he pulled out *Tomorrow and Tomorrow and Tomorrow* by Gabrielle Zenin, which, based on the title alone, intrigued Meghan. She'd adored reading Shakespeare in high school (because she'd been such a nerd, she supposed).

"It's an epic, of sorts," Daniel explained of Zenin's book. "Incredibly immersive. I'd say the central theme is a life-long friendship between two people, a woman and a man, who respect each other's minds so completely but never really fall in love."

Meghan tilted her head and accepted the book, which seemed like a tome compared to the other novels on the shelves. She took what he'd said about the book to be an incredible compliment, that he saw them on a tremendous path toward life-long friendship. It warmed her heart.

Meghan paid for the book, insisting that Daniel not give her the friends and family discount. "I want to support the store!" she said. Afterward, she clutched her new book to her chest and stood at the window alongside Daniel, watching as the snow piled up on the sidewalk and lined the naked limbs of trees.

"Can I ask you a question?" Meghan asked quietly, unable to look Daniel in the eye.

"Of course."

Meghan swallowed the lump in her throat. "Did you think your marriage was honest?"

Daniel gave her a sidelong glance that she couldn't possibly return. She fixated on the fire hydrant on the other side of the street, which now propped up two inches of fluffy white snow.

"For a long time, I thought it was," Daniel answered. "I couldn't believe that two people could be so close. I told her everything that came to my mind."

Meghan's heart thumped with memories of telling Hugo everything, of thinking they were nearly telepathic.

"What happened?" Meghan asked.

Daniel sighed. "It must have died off a little bit before we came to Martha's Vineyard. We raised our daughter together, which was lovely but exhausting, and I felt us drifting away from each other, but I genuinely couldn't think of a way to stop it. When I had to come to Martha's Vineyard to care for Mom, Gina initially told me to come alone. I begged her to come along, convinced the island would be the fresh start we needed.

"Anyway, I think part of our drifting had to do with our inability to be honest with each other about how we were feeling. If we had said something about it, alerted one another to our loneliness, maybe we could have salvaged it," Daniel continued.

Meghan reached out to touch Daniel on the shoulder, grateful for his honesty now. "It sounds like you really loved her."

"I still do," Daniel told her with a sad smile.

Meghan's hand dropped from his shoulder as she whispered, "What if my marriage wasn't honest from the start?"

Daniel's forehead worked itself into a big stack of wrinkles, not unlike the stack of books on his countertop. He stuttered, whispering, "What makes you say that?"

But Meghan's eyes were already thick with tears, and she couldn't speak any longer. Recognizing this conversation required a different kind of language, Daniel hurried behind the counter and retrieved two big chocolate chip cookies with sea salt. Meghan burst with a mix of tears and laughter.

"What is this?" she managed.

"It's me, bribing you into being my friend," Daniel tried to joke, his eyes tentative.

Meghan took a big, chocolatey bite, feeling the sharpness of the salt, the soft break of the dough, and the melting of the chocolate across her tongue. It was literally the best cookie of her life.

"I can't thank you enough for being here right now," Meghan said, blinking back more tears. "I was feeling so alone."

"Don't mention it," Daniel said softly. "I'm always here."

Chapter Nine

D aniel awoke on Monday morning to a text message from a number he didn't recognize.

> UNKNOWN: Hey! It's Meghan :). I finally
> got a new phone.

Daniel smiled to himself, shifting up onto his pillows as his heart pounded. Saturday afternoon, after she'd swung by the bookstore, he'd written his phone number down on a bookmark and pressed it into the book she'd purchased, which had felt very romantic, like something out of a nineties' sitcom. Daniel's thumbs were tentative over the screen, typing and deleting various ways of saying hello until he heard his mother creaking down the hallway and had to abandon his messages.

"You doing okay, Mom?" Daniel hustled up behind her, cursing himself for staying in bed too long.

His mother gave him a glance of annoyance. "I would be better if Lisa had taken out the trash like I asked her to."

Daniel sighed and sidled beside his mother, cupping her shoulder and touching her back as they ambled down the staircase. In the living room, he set her up with *The Golden Girls*, whom she'd begun to gossip about when the television wasn't on, as though they were people she actually knew and wasn't sure she liked. This was his mother's classic behavior. Regardless of who she'd come up against in life, she'd always found a way not to like them— including her own children.

As the coffee dripped into the pot, Daniel stretched his arms over his head, listening to his bones creak. Two slices of toast burst from the toaster, browned and warm, and he smeared them with peanut butter and margarine and delivered them to his mother. When he finally returned to the kitchen, he hunched over his cell phone again, his tongue poking out of his mouth as he wrote:

> DANIEL: Howdy! Congrats on the new phone.

> DANIEL: Have you started reading the book yet?

> MEGHAN: It's so good, Daniel! I haven't been able to put it down.

> MEGHAN: It's been a welcome distraction from everything going on in my life right now.

> MEGHAN: I'm sorry I've been so vague about that, by the way. Some of the stuff is too hard for me to say aloud. It hurts too much.

> DANIEL: I understand that more than most.

> DANIEL: I still find it difficult to say I'm getting divorced. I really thought we could make it work, you know? Part of me still believes that. Isn't that dumb?

> MEGHAN: It's not dumb. It's human nature.

> MEGHAN: It's what it means to be in love.

Daniel thought about Meghan all morning at the bookstore, watching the November winds blast against the glass of the Victorian and whip through the skeletal trees. It was two and a half weeks till Thanksgiving, a time that begged the question about whether he would celebrate or not. His mother didn't know what day it was and had never been so keen on holiday celebrations, anyway. But wasn't it depressing not to at least eat a bit extra that day? He grimaced, imagining himself eating a grilled cheese sandwich. It just wasn't right.

But around noon, as a stream of women in the local book club headed out, clutching their new purchases, Daniel received another surprise message on his phone. This one dropped him to the chair behind the counter, his heart in his throat.

> CAITLIN: Hey, Dad!

> CAITLIN: Can I call you?

Daniel's neck was slick with sweat. It had been months since he'd heard his daughter's voice, which put him in a state of panic. Perhaps there was something wrong. Perhaps Gina was sick or had gotten into an accident. Perhaps Caitlin's three-year-old son, Aidan, was ill.

Daniel braced himself and called Caitlin immediately. A question wavered in the back of his mind: *when had their relationship gotten so poisonous? And how could he fix it before it was too late?*

Caitlin answered on the second ring. "Hi." Her voice was sweet and soft, not unlike it had been when she was little, the tiniest girl in her preschool, underweight to the point that he and Gina had had to scramble to get her to eat more. Eventually, they'd discovered she adored onion rings (not exactly healthy, but a good amount of calories), and they'd given in to her desires for them at every turn until she grew a bit more. Every parent knew how strange it was to have children; every parent knew it wasn't as easy as forcing them to eat their vegetables.

"Caitlin! It's so good to hear your voice," Daniel said.

Caitlin sighed almost imperceptibly. "Yours, too. Listen. I have something to tell you. Something kind of crazy."

Daniel furrowed his brow, trying to parse her tone. It didn't sound like anyone was in grave danger, but it also didn't sound good.

"What's up?"

"I'm in Massachusetts," Caitlin explained. "Aiden and I flew here yesterday."

Daniel leaped from his chair, his blood pressure spiking. "You're out east?" His voice broke.

"Yeah. We're in a hotel outside of Boston."

In the background, Daniel thought he could hear his only grandson, Aiden, babbling happily. The last time he'd seen him, he hadn't been able to talk, although Caitlin had sent him a few photographs documenting his growth spurts: Aiden wearing her massive California sunglasses, Aiden at the beach, Aiden holding a large water bottle and giggling, squinting at the camera, Aiden eating and also covering himself in avocado.

"Come over to the Vineyard!" Daniel cried. "The ferry in Woods Hole is about an hour from Boston, and I can pick you up at the harbor. I'll even close the bookstore early."

Caitlin sounded hesitant. "I don't know if we can make it to the ferry."

"What?" There was something strange in Caitlin's voice, something resistant.

"I don't have a rental," Caitlin said.

"Can you call a cab?"

Caitlin sighed. "Money's an issue is all."

Daniel's heart rate spiked again. In his mind's eye, he streamed through the multiple bills he'd just typed into his spreadsheet that morning, proof of the weight of his mother's illness, the bookstore's rent, and the recent repairs on the house. On the one hand, he had very little to share; on the other, the only people in the world he wanted to share with were his daughter and grandson.

"I'll call a cab for you and pay over the phone," Daniel suggested. "Text me which hotel you're at, and I'll text you the details for the cab."

"Are you sure?" Caitlin asked.

"Of course." Daniel felt resolute. "I love you, honey."

"I love you, too." Caitlin stuttered as though wanted to add something to explain herself. But then, she muttered, "Bye," and hung up.

Daniel stared into space in stunned silence, cupping his phone. He had the sudden instinct to text Meghan about this, to explain just how much it meant for him to have his daughter visit. But before he gave into that, he read his daughter's information regarding her location, called a cab company on the outskirts of Boston, and set up transportation.

Meghan answered almost immediately, her voice warm and inviting over the phone. It felt as though a loving woman, someone who might have been his mother if his mother had ever been kind, wrapped him in a hug.

"How's your day going?" Meghan asked.

Daniel laughed. "I'm swimming in joy. And confusion." Quickly, Daniel explained that his daughter had hardly spoken to him since the divorce, that she'd spontaneously flown out east with her son. "What do you think she's doing here?"

"Huh. That's tricky." Meghan was quiet for a moment, and Daniel imagined her somewhere beautiful, perhaps in a book-filled room, twirling a pencil as she gazed at the Vineyard Sound out the window. "Do you think she got into a fight with your wife?"

"That's possible," Daniel said doubtfully. "Although they always got along so well. They were thick as thieves."

"My daughter and I always were, too," Meghan said. "But recently, we haven't been getting along. It happens." There was a twinge of sorrow behind her words, proof that what she said was just the tip of the iceberg.

"I'm sorry to hear that."

"This isn't about me," Meghan assured him. "This is about you and your daughter. Didn't you say she was married, too?"

"Yes," Daniel said, remembering Caitlin's husband, Brent, his broad forehead and his lack of bookshelves, his love of sports and only sports.

"You don't sound like you like him very much," Meghan said, a smile in her voice.

Katie Winters

"We aren't anything alike," Daniel explained. "But I have nothing against the guy."

"But he's not with them?"

"No," Daniel said, feeling hesitant. "Gosh, I'm getting more and more frightened. Something horrible must be going on. I hope I can help."

"You'll do the best you can. What time will they get here?"

"The ferry will arrive around four," Daniel answered. "I'm closing the bookstore to pick them up."

"You shouldn't close the store!" Meghan said. "Let me help. I can work from anywhere, you know. As long as you have Wi-Fi."

Daniel was floored. "I couldn't ask you to do that."

"I love that little store," Meghan assured him. "And I'm always looking for an excuse to get out of the house these days."

* * *

Daniel had always viewed himself as a practical person, a man with a good head on his shoulders. But as he showed Meghan around the bookstore, how to work the register, and where the keys and safe were located, he remembered he'd met Meghan less than a week ago— and wondered if he was going crazy. What man would put his pride and joy in the hands of a stranger?

As Daniel put on his winter coat and adjusted his scarf around his neck, he smiled back at Meghan, who stood happily at the counter with her laptop perched in front of her. He had a strange memory of his sister, Lisa, before she'd gone away, demanding of him, *"Why do you smile so much? I'll take that smile off your face for you."* She'd always accused him of being lost in the clouds.

"Good luck today," Meghan said. "You're going to be great."

Daniel sighed. "I don't feel great right now. But thank you."

Daniel waited in his car at the Oak Bluffs harbor, tapping his hands into a drumbeat on the steering wheel as the ferry sailed closer and closer, sidling against the cement dock. Workers in thick Carhartt coats and pants burst from the doorways to secure the vessel, and soon afterward, the few people coming to the island on a very cold Monday in November marched onto the dock. They played in contrast to the tourists of the summer, all of whom had laughed and smiled, wearing sundresses and khaki shorts and sunglasses, thrilled to be on vacation.

Daniel would have recognized Caitlin anywhere. She wore a long black peacoat and carried Aiden on her hip, frowning out across the harbor, looking for him. Daniel flung from the driver's side of his car and waved at her madly, feeling just as he had when he'd picked her up at kindergarten a million years ago. He'd wanted to save her from the barrage of other students, to take her home where she was safe.

The smile Caitlin gave him as she approached melted Daniel's heart. He threw his arms around both her and Aiden, feeling as though a piece of his heart was restored.

"Welcome to Martha's Vineyard!" Daniel cried, guiding them back toward his car.

Aiden jumped happily on Caitlin's hip as Caitlin explained, "This is your Grandpa, little guy. You remember him?"

It was clear Aiden didn't, which initially caused a

shadow to form over Daniel's heart. But, Daniel told himself, he now had a task at-hand: to make his grandson fall in love with him and to show him how much he cared. He took Aiden's little hand in his and said, "We're going to have a great time, aren't we, buddy?"

Because Daniel didn't have a car seat for Aiden, Caitlin sat in the backseat, holding onto Aiden tightly as Daniel drove slowly back to the house he'd been raised in. Caitlin had visited Daniel and Gina just once when they'd lived on the island together, mere months before Gina had left him and returned to California. Aiden had been one year old, adorably small and roly-poly, like the Pillsbury Dough Boy.

"It looks so different in winter," Caitlin commented as they drove past the Victorian homes, the historical streets, and the leaf-less trees and bushes.

"It still has magic to it," Daniel tried to assure her. "You just have to know how to find it."

"How's Grandma?" Caitlin asked as though she'd ever had a relationship with Pam— something Daniel had never even wanted her to have.

"She doesn't remember very much," Daniel said as he parked in the driveway and stopped the engine. "I don't know if she'll remember you."

"That's okay," Caitlin offered. "I hope us being here won't bother her too much?"

Daniel was touched by her care for her evil grandmother. "She'll be fine. We'll get used to each other." He had the urge to ask Caitlin how long she planned to stay, whether or not this was a three-day visit or a three-week visit. Could he get her to stay for Thanksgiving? Or was that pushing his luck?

As Daniel opened the door, Cindy, the nurse, bucked

up from the couch, where she'd clearly been slumbering. Daniel was too joyful to care.

"You can head home early, Cindy," he said. "Thanks for your help."

His mother was still in her nightgown, and she peered at Caitlin and little Aiden distrustfully. Aiden waddled around the living room as Caitlin hunted through her backpack to retrieve a granola bar and a few toys for Aiden to play with. Very soon, Aiden gummed through the granola bar and drove a large plastic truck over the dining room floor, making vrooming noises. It was music to Daniel's ears.

"You packed light," Daniel said to Caitlin, feeling about as useless in the conversation department as he had last week on his date.

"I didn't want to check a bag," Caitlin explained, collapsing at the kitchen table and rubbing her temples. At twenty-six, she looked older than she ever had, with bags under her eyes. Having a toddler was intense.

"What do you want for dinner?" Daniel asked.

"Oh, gosh, Dad. I don't care."

"Why don't we order burgers? Do you still like onion rings?"

Caitlin's eyes sparkled for only a moment, proof that somewhere in there was Daniel's little girl. "Sounds good."

When the burgers arrived, Daniel set the table and removed the packaging, watching as Caitlin cleaned Aiden's hands in the sink with soap and water.

"Is she going to join us?" Caitlin asked under her breath.

"She doesn't like burgers," Daniel explained. "I'll make her something else after this." He didn't want to go into the fact that his mother didn't have much of an appetite these days, that he'd had to go through a multi-month era of trial and error to figure out what would keep her alive.

Caitlin sat at the table with Aiden on her lap, blinking down at the burgers and onion rings. Daniel hadn't been able to help himself; he'd sprung for milkshakes, too—strawberry for Caitlin and chocolate for himself. As Caitlin reached for an onion ring and raised it, her lower lip began to jump around, and her eyes filled with tears.

"Oh, honey. What's wrong?" Daniel's heart sank. Had he done something wrong?

Caitlin chewed and swallowed the onion ring, her face etched with sorrow. "I just don't know what to do, Dad."

Daniel shoved his burger to the side, wanting to be her superhero, to be the one who took all this pain away.

"It just seems like there's so much wrong with our family," Caitlin went on, her voice edged with drama. "Like no matter how hard I try, I can't get away from it."

Daniel tilted his head with surprise. "Did something happen back in California?"

"I mean, obviously!" Caitlin cried, then snapped her hand over her mouth. "I'm sorry," she muttered. "I don't know what's wrong with me. I don't know how to act right now."

Daniel nodded and stared at the table, recognizing the dramatic distance between them. It was true that he and Caitlin had never had an open and honest conversation, that Caitlin had reserved those for Gina. But why wasn't Caitlin talking to Gina about whatever this was? Why was she here?

Daniel was reminded of his sister, Lisa, of the drama

she'd brought to his everyday life, of the fact that he'd always been at the mercy of her moods— tiptoeing around her when she'd gotten into a fight with her boyfriend or their mother. Just now, with Caitlin scowling at her onion rings, unable to articulate what was wrong, she looked surprisingly like his sister. Daniel tried to shake the image from his mind.

"I'm here for you, honey," he said softly. "Whatever it is, we can work through it. Together."

Caitlin sighed and took another onion ring. After another long pause (all of which nearly stopped Daniel's heart from beating), she said, "These are delicious, Dad. Thank you. And thank you for picking us up today. It means the world."

"You know I'm here for you," Daniel said, palming the back of his neck. "You know I love you more than anything."

Chapter Ten

More than twenty years ago, Meghan had taught Hugo the rules of day trading, giving tips and tricks to ensure their family's income would be robust until retirement. Since then, Meghan and Hugo had mostly worked separately, frequently competing with one another on who could make the most profits, thinking of it as a healthy race—one that pushed their intellect and their skills. Now that Meghan wanted as much distance from Hugo as possible, however, she refused to discuss how her work was going, always ate her meals alone in her study, and slept in the guest bedroom. She was enraged and alienated from her life. More than that, she was frightened that the minute Hugo touched her again or spoke to her as though nothing was wrong, she would burst into tears.

Hugo sensed the distance between them. He walked around the house like a wounded animal, his eyes showing his terror of her. It made her want to scream.

But Tuesday afternoon, Meghan made a grave error— one that, she knew, probably cut her month's profits down by a third. Stricken, she placed her hand over her heart and gaped out the window, genuinely surprised. It wasn't like her to trade so flippantly. She often analyzed her strategy upwards of ten times before making a decision.

She had the sudden instinct to run to Hugo's study and sob to him about her mistake, which she resented. She couldn't let her emotions get the better of her, not now and not when she worked. She raised her chin and gave herself an internal pep talk, then decided to take the rest of the day off. If she was really going to make mistakes like this, she wasn't safe at her computer.

Meghan entered her walk-in closet, a separate entity from Hugo's walk-in closet, filled with linen pants, soft white blouses, and floral dresses. In the back was a shelf laden with her yoga clothes and tight spandex outfits that made her feel athletic and sleek. She donned a black onesie and pulled her short hair into a sharp ponytail, then grabbed her yoga mat and headed back to her study.

But on her way, Hugo leaped from his study and stood between her and her destination. His eyes were large and wounded, and he spoke with the confidence of someone who'd been preparing for this meeting all morning.

"Meghan," he stuttered, eyeing her yoga mat and outfit with clear interest. "Is there something you want to talk to me about?"

Meghan pressed her tongue into her inner cheek. Of course, this was her opening to blare: *why are you a liar?* But it didn't feel tactful.

"Why?" Meghan asked.

Hugo's forehead glistened with nervous sweat. "You haven't slept in our bedroom in almost a week. You won't eat with me. You barely look at me." Hugo sputtered. "What did I do, Meghan? Please, can you tell me?"

Meghan raised her shoulders flippantly.

Hugo stared at the ground, and the silence threatened to drown them.

"Are you falling in love with someone else?" Hugo whispered.

"What?" Meghan's voice was sharp.

"You can tell me," Hugo went on. "It's not like I haven't noticed you texting all the time. You're always buried in your phone, writing to someone."

Meghan rolled her eyes. "Don't be ridiculous."

"We can work through this," Hugo said, his voice urgent. "Whatever it is. We're strong, Meghan. We always have been."

There was a creak on the staircase, and Meghan and Hugo turned as Theo appeared, looking sheepish. He unwound his scarf from his neck, his eyes flickering between his parents. He looked worried, as though he thought he'd just walked into the discussion about the letters.

"Hey," he said finally. "Is now a bad time?"

Hugo combed through his gray-and-black curls with his fingers. "Hey, Theo. I forgot about our meeting."

"I can come back another time," Theo insisted, stepping back down the stairs.

"No," Meghan insisted. "Your father has plenty of time. Come on up."

Theo blinked up at them, looking like a little kid. Meghan walked around Hugo and scurried for her office, clipping the door closed behind her. For a moment, she remained standing, listening intently as Theo finally crept up the staircase.

"Do you know what's going on with your mother?" Hugo asked softly, not wanting to be heard.

"I don't know anything," Theo said quickly, adding to his lies.

"I've never seen her like this," Hugo admitted, his voice cracking. He sounded on the verge of tears.

"Are you sure you want to work today?" Theo asked, itching to go. "We can meet another day this week."

"No." Hugo sighed as he crept back toward his office. "I don't want to be alone right now. If you stay, you'll be doing me a favor."

Meghan collapsed on the yoga mat and stared at the ceiling, listening as Hugo closed his study door, enclosing him and Theo in their separate world of day trading. Her stomach tightened and released at the shame she felt at making the work mistake earlier, proof her mind was elsewhere.

Before she committed herself to an hour of yoga, Meghan grabbed her new cell and texted Daniel.

> MEGHAN: How's it going with your daughter?

> DANIEL: She's clearly upset about something, but she won't tell me what.

> DANIEL: She brought Aiden to the bookstore today, though. I'm thrilled they're here.

> DANIEL: But I feel like I'm walking on eggshells.

> MEGHAN: She needs you right now. It sounds like you're giving her the moral support she needs.

DANIEL: I hope so. How are things at your house?

MEGHAN: The mess is just getting messier.

DANIEL: :(

DANIEL: Can I help somehow?

MEGHAN: Can you build a time machine and take me back to twenty-seven years ago?

DANIEL: If only. I was twenty-three years old, living in California, at the top of my game.

DANIEL: I can't say I feel at the top of anything right now.

MEGHAN: Me neither. I just made a professional mistake that cost me thousands.

DANIEL: Ugh. I don't know what to say.

MEGHAN: Just say I'm an idiot.

DANIEL: I haven't met anyone as intelligent and kind as you in a very long time.

DANIEL: Remember that.

Chapter Eleven

After Tuesday's professional error, Meghan rebounded as best as she could. She woke up early, did yoga, ate healthy food, avoided alcohol, and continued to avoid Hugo— insisting to herself that one day, she would discover a way to approach him about what he'd done. That day never seemed to be today.

Meghan agreed to meet Oriana Friday afternoon. It had been a little while since they'd seen one another, as Oriana had been in New York City handling an art deal. Oriana had invited Meghan to come with her, as was her custom, but Meghan hadn't felt up to such a journey, feeling unable to carry the weight of her broken heart with her.

They met at a boutique downtown, a favorite of theirs since they'd turned forty and realized their styles needed to change. (Meghan had been perfectly fine to see her thirty-something styles go by the wayside, to make way for more practical clothing. Oriana had struggled.) As Meghan opened the boutique door, Oriana hurried forward to hug her, bringing with her a wave of dark perfume with a hint of vanilla.

"I'm so glad to be back!" Oriana sighed. "This trip wasn't one of the fun ones."

"What happened?" Meghan asked.

Oriana launched into an explanation about her recent art deal, which had very nearly failed as a result of the client's inability to understand what was good and what wasn't. "Or maybe it's just me," Oriana said as she flicked through dresses on the nearest rack, shaking her head. "Maybe I'm out of touch with the current art trends."

"I don't think so," Meghan insisted. "Just because one client disagrees with you doesn't mean you should second-guess what's good."

"It's hard to feel confident in your opinions every second of the day," Oriana offered, her voice wavering.

Meghan nodded, dropping her gaze. "I made a huge mistake the other day. I couldn't believe it. I hadn't made an error like that in something like twenty years."

"Oh no." Oriana winced. "I'm so sorry to hear that. What did Hugo say?"

"I didn't tell him." Meghan's voice hardened, and she disappeared around another rack of clothing, peering down at a selection of leather boots that she wasn't particularly interested in.

Oriana followed her. "Is there something going on between you and Hugo?"

Meghan refused to look at Oriana; she was frightened Oriana would be able to see all the pain and torment in her eyes, clear as day. "What? Why do you say that?"

"I was previously under the impression that you and Hugo told each other everything," Oriana said.

"Oh? Well, we don't."

Oriana clucked her tongue and picked up one of the leather boots to look at the wooden bottom. It was four sizes too big for her, but she was too distracted to notice.

"You didn't tell Reese what was going on with the blackmailer," Meghan pointed out.

"I didn't want him to worry," Oriana said.

"And I don't want Hugo to think I'm an idiot. Simple as that."

Oriana returned the boot to the shelf. "Hugo thinks you're brilliant. We all do." She bit her lower lip, staining her teeth with fire hydrant red lipstick. "Everyone makes mistakes, Meghan. Remember mine? I sold a three-million-dollar forged painting to a client?"

"That wasn't your fault," Meghan said.

"I should have noticed."

Meghan sighed, sensing she wouldn't win this argument, and pointed at her own teeth. "You have lipstick on your two front teeth."

Oriana groaned and hurried toward the nearest mirror to clean up, allowing Meghan to make a quick escape toward the accessories. Although it was winter, she donned a pair of oversized sunglasses and imagined herself getting on a plane, flying across the country to California, and starting a new life. Maybe she could introduce herself with a different name— Tiffany, Lola, or Naomi.

"You never told me what happened last week." Oriana appeared beside her again, removing a pair of earrings from the hanger and pulling them up to her ear, assessing the way they matched her hair and skin tone. "When you came back to The Jessabelle House."

Meghan crossed her arms. "I told you. I just went for a long walk and got really cold."

Oriana gave her a look that proved she didn't believe her, not in the slightest. "Eva and Theo looked upset, too."

"Parents fight with their children," Meghan reminded her easily. "I wasn't happy with them, and they weren't happy with me."

"But you've made up since then, haven't you?"

Meghan made a beeline for the front door, sweeping through her list of available excuses, on the hunt for a way out of this Friday excursion with her sister. Could she say she wasn't feeling well? That she had a headache?

"Hey!" Oriana hurried up behind her. "It's five o'clock. Why don't we swing by the wine bar? I'd love a snack and a glass of Cab." Oriana touched Meghan's shoulder, forcing Meghan's eyes toward her as she added, "I don't mean to pry, Sis. Okay? I just love you. I'm just worried."

Meghan raised her shoulder, willing herself to make an excuse. But Oriana's eyes begged her to make peace, and so she said, "Okay. A glass of Cab sounds good."

As they walked to the wine bar, November gusts burst through them, tearing at their coats and hats. Islanders out for an early Friday evening scurried in and out of their vehicles, their cheeks red with cold.

"Can you believe Thanksgiving is still two weeks away?" Oriana cried as they turned the corner and headed for the wine bar. "It already feels like December!"

Meghan's stomach twisted with sorrow at the Thanksgiving topic. Never in her life had she dreaded that gorgeous, family-filled holiday. Now, she wasn't sure how to face it.

But suddenly, through the taut and frigid air came the sound of someone calling her name.

"Meghan! Hey!"

Meghan and Oriana whipped around to find Daniel, a young woman in her twenties pushing a stroller, and a very old woman, all bundled up and heading in their direction. Daniel looked happier than Meghan had seen him, wearing a perpetual smile, hurrying toward her with his arms extended.

"Oh! Hi!" Meghan laughed and hugged Daniel back, her cheeks warm with embarrassment.

"Caitlin, this is my friend, Meghan. And Meghan, this is my daughter, Caitlin, my grandson, Aiden, and my mother, Pam."

Meghan waved timidly, noting that Daniel's mother peered off in the distance, uninterested.

"We're going to visit my daughter," Pam explained flatly.

Daniel ignored her, clearly accustomed to his mother's fictions. He peered at Oriana happily and said, "Oriana, right?"

Oriana's lips formed a perfect O. "Goodness! You look familiar."

"We were in the same class in high school," Daniel explained, stuttering slightly, clearly embarrassed that he'd remembered Oriana and she hadn't in return. "But I wouldn't have been on your radar, I guess."

"I didn't even think to ask if you knew my sister," Meghan said with a laugh. "Oriana, Daniel and I just met last week in the wine bar. He was away for many years in California, but he just moved back a couple of years ago to open The White Whale Bookstore."

"I see," Oriana said, then slid her tongue over her

teeth. She looked at Daniel as though she didn't trust him.

"She's waiting for us," Pam said to Daniel, clearly annoyed.

"We're on our way to an early dinner," Daniel explained. "I had someone fill in for me at the bookstore today."

"Wonderful. You need to give yourself more time off," Meghan told him.

"That's what I said," Caitlin offered, smiling nervously, and glancing at her father. She looked as though she loved him but also wasn't sure about him, as though she was experiencing whiplash after her spontaneous trip.

"I hope you enjoy it," Meghan said. "We should all get out of the cold."

After they said their goodbyes, Meghan and Oriana walked in silence the rest of the way to the wine bar, where they were seated near the window so they could watch the beginnings of a snowfall. Oriana gripped her menu with white-tipped fingers and gaped at Meghan, her cheeks slack.

"What's up?" Meghan asked. She still felt warm from their encounter with Daniel, as though she'd just seen a family member she hadn't seen in a while.

"You met that guy last week? At this wine bar?" Oriana asked.

Meghan raised her shoulders. "It's a funny story. He was on a horrible date with that woman, Victoria. I think you met her at that volunteer thing last year. Anyway, I was eavesdropping on their conversation until Victoria got up, told him he needed to lose weight, and stormed out."

Oriana's jaw dropped further down. "He isn't overweight at all!"

"Victoria always goes for the jugular," Meghan said. "Anyway, he completely broke down after that, and I sat with him for a while to try to cheer him up."

Oriana nodded as though she was trying to comprehend something very complex. "Was he ever married?"

"He's getting divorced," Meghan explained. "Well, his wife wants to divorce, but he's struggling to sign the divorce papers. Do you want to share the spinach and artichoke dip?"

Oriana wasn't ready to discuss the menu. "He looked at you like he was in love with you."

Meghan scoffed. "That's ridiculous. We've only known each other a bit longer than a week."

"He has a crush on you," Oriana said.

Meghan shifted in her chair and dropped the menu. She wasn't sure what to say. "I was there for him when he was having a hard time. That's all."

"He's obviously lonely," Oriana whispered so as not to be overheard in the bar. "And, if I remember correctly, he was never great with women back in high school. You giving him attention is probably enough to make him fall for you."

"Are you suggesting that women and men can't be friends?" Meghan asked, raising a single eyebrow.

"This isn't *When Harry Met Sally*." Oriana shook her head, smiling slowly. "I have plenty of male friends, and I adore them. I just want you to be careful. The way Daniel looks at you scares me."

Meghan closed her eyes as resentment crystallized in her chest. For a long time, she pressed down on what she wanted to say until it came pouring out of her like lava.

"Why does nobody think I can handle anything myself? Do I have 'idiot' written across my forehead? Do I appear weak?"

Oriana's eyes glinted with surprise. "What do you mean?"

"I mean, I know how to handle my friendships. I know how to handle the truth. I'm an adult woman." Meghan spoke quickly, her anger rising. "I don't need your advice about Daniel. Or about anything else!"

Oriana stared down at the table, looking as though she'd been slapped. "I'm sorry."

Meghan's anger dissipated just as quickly as it had appeared. "It's okay."

"No. I know. You would never go behind Hugo's back. You would never have an inappropriate friendship with another man," Oriana said, waving her hand. "You're my sister. I know exactly who you are."

Meghan remained wordless, scanning the menu again without fully comprehending what it said.

"Who else doesn't think you can handle things?" Oriana asked. "I mean, where is all this anger coming from?"

Meghan rolled her shoulders back as the faces of Hugo, Eva, and Theo floated in her mind's eye.

"It doesn't matter," she insisted.

Oriana gave her a final confused look just as the waiter approached to take their order. Meghan forced her voice to brighten, pretending she was a woman without a care in the world. After the waiter left, Oriana let her get away with it, at least for now, and chatted about anything else that came into her mind— avoiding Meghan's personal woes as though they were landmines.

Chapter Twelve

Late that evening, long after both Daniel's mother and his grandson were fast asleep upstairs, Daniel was cozied up in an easy chair, reading while his daughter wrote in a journal. They'd been like this, spending quiet time together, for nearly two hours at this point, neither one of them willing to interrupt the silence for mundane conversation. It had been a long time since Daniel had felt so comfortable with someone; his shoulders had lost their tightness, and he breathed easily.

Suddenly, Caitlin's phone buzzed on the end table. Daniel couldn't help but glance its way, noting the name of the caller: BRENT, Caitlin's husband. To Daniel's surprise, Caitlin reached over, cut the call, and continued to write in her journal as though nothing had happened. Daniel coughed twice, purring with confusion. *Why was Caitlin avoiding Brent's calls? Had they not spoken at all since Caitlin had come out east?*

If Daniel had been Brent, he would have been worried sick— not only for Caitlin's sake but for his son's.

Daniel took a long, deep breath, closed his book, and said, "Honey, what's going on with you and Brent?"

Caitlin glared at him over her journal, looking every bit like the teenager she'd once been. "I don't want to talk to him. That's all."

Daniel's stomach twisted. The beautiful silence they'd shared was now destroyed.

"But don't you think he's worried about you?" Daniel suggested.

Caitlin raised her shoulders. "I don't really care what he's thinking."

"Oh, honey. What did he do to you?" Daniel tore through his mind for the best way to handle this, wondering if he should call Brent himself and demand what he'd done.

Caitlin's chin wiggled as she blinked back tears. "It's not like he hit me or anything."

Daniel breathed a sigh of relief. That was every father's nightmare.

"But I never want to see or speak to him ever again," Caitlin went on. "He's as good as dead to me."

"Married couples fight," Daniel said quietly, remembering his own spats with Gina— the ones they'd had to have throughout their many years of marriage, almost as a way to prove to one another how much they wanted to fight for their love.

"And sometimes, married couples break up," Caitlin responded. "You and Mom did."

"But we were married for a very long time," Daniel reminded her. "And throughout that time, we had many arguments, all of which we found a way to get through. As a team."

Caitlin snorted and stared out the window, which was inky black and dotted with fluttering snow.

"So, you got into a fight? And then flew here?" Daniel asked quietly. "Is that why you didn't want to use your credit card for the taxi? Because you didn't want him to know where you were?"

Caitlin shrugged. "He never would have guessed we'd come all the way out here."

Daniel's heart dropped into his stomach. This was beyond his own comprehension. Obviously, Caitlin had wanted to run to her mother for protection in the wake of this argument— but she'd known Brent would find her there. Daniel was a consolation prize, a secret.

"Honey, I've told you about my sister, haven't I?" Daniel began, his voice breaking.

Caitlin stared at the ground, her eyes glinting with tears. She looked on the edge of falling apart.

"When Lisa was twenty-five, she cut contact with everyone she'd ever known and left the island," Daniel went on. "I was twenty-three at the time and so, so lost without her. She'd been very cruel to me growing up, but that didn't mean I didn't love her. I think that she was only cruel because our mother was so awful to us. And I knew, of course, that my mother was only cruel because our father had left her."

"So much pain," Caitlin whispered to the ground. "There's no way out of it."

Daniel wanted to protest, to tell his daughter that he had been very careful not to pass any of his family's pain down to her, his only child. But what did he know? Maybe he had, accidentally. Maybe the pain had woven its way through little phrases he'd used, or his facial expressions, or his tone of voice. It was impossible to get out of the web of family genetics.

Instead, Daniel said, "When my mom got really sick, I looked for Lisa again. Technology has gone through leaps and bounds since the nineties, so I figured I'd be able to reach out to her, tell her our mother was sick, and ask her for help. I imagined us balancing the work to ensure that I could maintain my life in California, and she could keep doing whatever the heck she was doing. But I couldn't find her. Lisa basically disappeared off the face of the planet. And do you know what?"

Caitlin frowned.

"I think, even though my mother is a very sad and messed up person, Lisa leaving like that shattered her," Daniel continued. "Nobody knows what to do when someone disappears like that. And that's what you're doing to Brent."

Caitlin suddenly stood up, shoved her phone into her pocket, and set her jaw. "I didn't come here for advice, Dad."

Daniel's heart pounded. Had he gone too far— so far that Caitlin would end their relationship for good? It was certainly possible. But this was something he felt really passionate about, something that mattered.

"I just don't think the mistakes of the past need to be repeated, is all," Daniel said quietly. "Making yourself disappear isn't kind. It hurts people."

Caitlin pulled her hair into a tight ponytail and closed her eyes. Daniel felt as though his words crashed into her, over and over, their power strengthening in the silence.

"I'm going to bed," Caitlin said, her tone harsh.

Daniel swallowed the lump in his throat, cursing

himself. "If Aiden wakes up, I can take care of him," he said, hoping this was a way to calm Caitlin's anger.

"I got it," Caitlin shot back, turning to go up the staircase. "I don't need help."

For a good half-hour, Daniel sat in stunned silence, his book on his lap and his ears ringing with shock. The fight had happened all at once, coming from seemingly nothing. Perhaps he'd just destroyed the only family relationship he had left. And for what? For Brent's feelings? Daniel felt like a fool.

Before he knew what he was doing, he called Meghan, already thinking of her as his lighthouse in the storm. She answered, just as she always did. It occurred to him, now, that she still hadn't told him why she thought her marriage was so dishonest. Did she just not trust him?

Daniel explained what had happened with his daughter, along with his fears that she would pack her bag in the middle of the night and take off.

"She doesn't have anywhere else to go," Meghan assured him softly. "She needs you. She just hates admitting it."

"She's stubborn," Daniel breathed. "Maybe she gets that from me."

Meghan laughed gently. "Do you think you'll be able to sleep?"

"No way," Daniel said. The idea of laying back on his mattress was alienating. Besides, he'd resolved to stay up and wait by the door, if only to ensure Caitlin didn't leave before he woke up.

Oh, it felt awful to think of her doing that. If she did, Daniel would be left alone with the mother who'd once hated him and didn't remember him. What a miserable life that was.

"I can come over," Meghan whispered. "If you want company."

Daniel watched at the window for the full fifteen minutes it took Meghan to drive from wherever it was she lived with her husband, a mystery man she'd hardly mentioned. When her car appeared at the end of the driveway, she shut the lights and brought her vehicle to a crawl.

Daniel hurried to the kitchen to put the kettle on, thinking they could have hot cocoa. But when he opened the door for Meghan, as the kettle bubbled and spat, Meghan raised a bottle of wine through the darkness and said, "Tonight calls for a glass." Daniel didn't have any alcohol in the house— and his shoulders fell forward with gratitude.

Out on the enclosed porch that overlooked the street, Daniel and Meghan wrapped themselves up in blankets, sipped wine, and spoke in soft tones. Daniel burned to ask Meghan where her husband thought she was so late at night, whether or not she'd told him about their budding friendship. Occasionally, he questioned his own narrative, asking himself if he was falling for Meghan. But each time he looked at her, he felt only waves of trustfulness and hope— as though she was the sunrise after a horrific all-night storm.

Daniel was talking to Meghan about his sister, about how she'd broken his mother's heart.

"It doesn't make logical sense," he explained. "My mother was nothing but cruel to her when she lived here. But as soon as she disappeared, my mother acted like the biggest victim. She cried so much. Her full cruelty went to me after that. And I just couldn't stand it. It's why I went to California. I still called once a week, though. I didn't want to completely disappear."

"That's terrible." Meghan sipped her wine thoughtfully. "And you still have no idea where your sister wound up?"

"Haven't heard from her since she was twenty-five years old," Daniel said. "Which is bizarre to me. That's one year younger than Caitlin is right now. You would think, after so many years of getting older and more mature, she would have reached out. My mother still lives in the same house. We still have that landline!"

"Plus, there's social media to consider," Meghan added.

"So many different ways to reach out," Daniel affirmed, still flabbergasted. "I just don't want Caitlin to abandon people the way Lisa abandoned us. It isn't right."

Meghan turned her head slowly and lowered her wine, blinking slowly. The look on her face was difficult to read, although, initially, Daniel thought she was sizing him up.

"I'm sorry," Meghan whispered. "What did you say your sister's name was?"

"Lisa," Daniel said. "Lisa Bloom."

Meghan's gaze slid away from him. She cast it out into the thick darkness, her lips parted.

"Did you know her?" Daniel asked. "She must have been five years ahead of you in school, so I figured there was no way."

Meghan swallowed a large gulp of wine. "I never knew her," she said in a small voice.

"But you've heard the name before?"

Meghan shook her head a little too quickly, her hair

tossing back and forth over her ears. "Never heard it, no." She downed the rest of her wine and placed the glass on the porch table, her hand shaking.

"Meghan, are you okay?" Daniel was on high alert, wondering if he'd said yet another destructive thing that evening. He felt like a bull in a china shop.

"I'm fine," Meghan answered, although that was clearly a lie. "I'd better be going. I don't like to drive on more than one glass."

"Of course." Daniel stood, his heart thudding, and reached for her coat on the rack. "Do you want anything before you go? I made some cookies for Aidan yesterday."

"You're too kind," Meghan whispered, shrugging her coat onto her shoulders. "But I can't eat as many cookies as a three-year-old."

Daniel tried to laugh, although it sounded unnatural in his own ears. "Me neither. I wish I could. Drive home safe, okay?" He extended his arms for a hug, which Meghan agreed to briefly before stepping back and heading for the door. Daniel watched her, his hands hanging sadly at his sides, until her car picked up speed toward the end of the block and turned the corner. He wondered, with what felt like rocks in his gut, if he would ever see her again. And he had no idea what he'd done wrong.

Chapter Thirteen

The drive back to her home on the coast was a difficult one. Meghan's vision was blurry, with streetlamp lights like big glowing orbs and car beamers like long, glowing streams. When Meghan finally parked her car in the garage, directly next to Hugo's, she placed her forehead on the steering wheel and willed herself not to scream. She couldn't alarm Hugo like that.

Meghan tip-toed through the garage entrance, listening for signs of Hugo in the house. After a few seconds, she heard a cough from the basement, where Hugo sometimes liked to watch sports by himself, and Meghan breathed a sigh of relief. He didn't seem keen on running upstairs to ask where she'd been. He knew to leave her alone.

Meghan changed into her pajamas in her walk-in closet, too exhausted to do anything but throw her jeans and sweater to the ground. As she walked toward her study, she felt as though she walked the plank. And by the time she returned to the stack of letters from Hugo's ex-fiancé, she'd nearly worked herself into a panic attack.

Every single one of the letters had been signed:

Yours forever,

Lisa

Meghan's head pounded with fear. Was it possible that Hugo's Lisa was also Daniel's Lisa? It felt like too much of a coincidence— but then again, on such a small island, coincidences were a way of life. Lisa was five years older than Meghan, as was Hugo. They'd obviously gone to high school at the same time. They'd grown up together.

It was more than likely this was the Lisa of the letters.

Many, many years ago, when Eva had been six months old and sick with a terrifying fever, Hugo and Meghan had stayed up all night, ready to go to the hospital at any point. To distract themselves, Hugo and Meghan had shown off their old yearbooks, laughing at photographs of Meghan with braces and Hugo with long, hippie hair, which he'd sported at the age of sixteen. Meghan had graduated in 1994, which meant Hugo had graduated in 1989— another decade entirely, with completely different music and styles.

Meghan and Hugo kept their yearbooks in Hugo's study, a room Meghan hadn't entered since before she'd discovered the letters. Entering it now felt like walking into the past. The desk was piled with work papers and empty mugs that had once contained coffee, and— most notably— there was a book on the chair in the corner entitled *Marriage is Work: Be the Best Partner You Can Be.*

Oh, Hugo, she wanted to tell him. *It's already too late.*

Meghan removed Hugo's 1989 yearbook from the shelf, listening intently for his footfalls on the staircase. Her heart filling with terror, she opened the yearbook to the senior page, where she skimmed past handsome Hugo

Porter, the man she'd loved for decades, and landed upon Lisa Bloom. The young woman in the photograph was eighteen years old, still a girl in so many ways, with blond hair that streamed down her shoulders, a confident smile, and a light in her eyes. Sure, Meghan could have been jealous of this young woman. But what did it mean if Meghan was jealous of an eighteen-year-old?

Daniel had said Lisa had disappeared at the age of twenty-five, seven years after this photograph was taken. Meghan flipped to the very last page of the yearbook, where students had written well-wishes for Hugo, saying things like, "See you this summer!" and, "Congrats, Class of '89!" and, "This summer, we're going to start a band and get famous." Some of them made Meghan's lips curl into a near-smile, proof of her constant love for this man and everything he stood for.

That's when she found Lisa Bloom's message and her smile fell.

It was the same handwriting as in the letters, yet perhaps with a more youthful flourish. Lisa had written:

"I cannot wait to move in with you this summer, marry you, and have your babies, Hugo Porter. You are my greatest gift. I would be lost without you. Love, Lisa Bloom." She'd drawn a flower and a heart beside it.

Meghan stared at the words for a long time. When she swallowed and breathed again, she found that her tongue tasted like sand.

The math had begun to add up.

Meghan had met Hugo when he was twenty-five. Lisa had disappeared at the age of twenty-five.

But when had Lisa and Hugo broken up? Hugo hadn't mentioned any girlfriend or ex-girlfriend, not the first night they'd kissed at the abandoned hotel, and not any of their dates afterward. Meghan had been pregnant within six months, for crying out loud, and he'd never mentioned that, very recently, his childhood sweetheart and first love had literally disappeared from the island.

Hugo's office had begun to shift around her. Meghan felt horribly dizzy and on the verge of throwing up, and she quickly returned the yearbook to the shelf and entered the guest bedroom, which she immediately locked. For a long time, she sat at the edge of the bed and gazed out at the moon, wondering if she'd just stumbled into something truly horrific.

One thought splintered everything.

What if Hugo had had something to do with Lisa's disappearance?

What if she hadn't run off the island for greener pastures, never to be seen or heard from again?

Lisa's heart seized with shock and terror, and she fell back against the mattress, quivering. It was impossible, wasn't it?

Then again, Meghan had read countless stories just like this one: wherein a woman discovered the truth about the man she'd loved for decades, that he'd murdered someone in the past, or that he'd robbed a bank, or that he'd committed fraud. People always regarded the woman in the story with pity. "How couldn't she have known she was sleeping next to a monster?"

But Meghan had never suspected anything. Not once. Now, was she the fool?

Chapter Fourteen

Caitlin was icy with Daniel for the majority of that Sunday, hardly looking him in the eye as they fell into a makeshift routine: taking Aiden and Daniel's mother for a walk, eating lunch, and watching television as the snow fell. Although Daniel felt weak with sorrow, he was grateful she hadn't stormed out and made herself scarce in his life. Maybe Meghan had been right: Caitlin didn't have anywhere else to go.

Aiden went to bed every night at seven, which necessitated a bath and reading time. For whatever reason, tonight, Aiden begged that his grandfather be the one to do bath time and reading. For the first time, Caitlin looked at him, a near smile on her lips. "Does Grandpa have time?"

"I have time," Daniel assured them both, his heart heaving with love for the little boy. As he helped him in the bath, listening to the splash of the water and Aiden's bright giggles, he realized just how useful he felt. His mother needed him, his daughter needed him, and his grandson needed him. It was a pretty wonderful feeling.

After Aiden collapsed into a deep sleep on Daniel's chest, Daniel closed the picture book slowly and lay there for a little while. Aiden's breath was soft and clean, and his little belly rose and fell adorably. Had Gina been there, she would have gushed about how cute he was. Abstractly, Daniel wondered if Caitlin was keeping in contact with her mother while she was here. Because he hadn't heard from Gina at all, he guessed Caitlin was.

Before he crawled out of Aiden's bed, he opened his chat with Meghan, who hadn't written at all that day. She'd left in a rush the night before, terrifying him. What had caused it? He still wasn't sure.

> DANIEL: Are you okay?

> DANIEL: You made it home all right last night, didn't you?

> MEGHAN: I'm okay.

> MEGHAN: I have something to talk to you about.

Daniel's stomach seized with worry. Did she think he was hitting on her, that he was bent on destroying her marriage? The idea made him dizzy with sickness. Of course, the sad, lonely part of him had enjoyed the way she'd looked at him, as though he was the only man in the world. But that was probably just a projection he'd created in his mind.

> DANIEL: Okay. I'll be at the bookstore tomorrow from nine to seven. Come by any time.

Daniel struggled to sleep that night. He tried to read, to turn on the television in his bedroom, but no distraction helped guide him into unconsciousness. When he woke up the next morning, he forced himself to care for his mother, eat breakfast, and shower, but everything felt heavy with anxiety about what came next. What did Meghan want to talk about?

The answer came around one-thirty that afternoon. Daniel was hard at work, shelving new boxes of books he'd received in time for Black Friday, grateful for something to think about besides his own terror. That's when Meghan appeared in the doorway, bringing with her a wave of November chill. She didn't smile, and her face was blotchy with tears.

"Meghan!" Daniel cried, nearly dropping his book. "Are you all right?"

Meghan's lower lip quivered. She glanced through the bookstore, which was mostly empty except for a twenty-something couple in the corner, both reading graphic novels.

"Can we talk in the back?" she asked.

Daniel was hesitant, if only because the twenty-somethings hadn't yet paid, and he was fearful they would leave without doing so. Still, his friendship with Meghan, even though it was still new, meant much more than that revenue, so he led her into the backroom, where she collapsed in the cushioned chair and bent over her thighs to cup her chin with her hands. Daniel remained standing, frightened that if he sat down, he wouldn't manage to get back up again.

"My husband was engaged to your sister," Meghan announced, obviously uninterested in beating around the bush.

Daniel's jaw dropped. "What are you talking about?"

Meghan's eyes were heavy with despair. "My husband is Hugo Porter. I'm sure you've met him."

Daniel's stomach tightened into knots, and he collapsed in his computer chair. Memories crashed into one another, a barrage of images: Hugo and Lisa walking in front of Daniel, holding hands. Hugo and Lisa driving him to the movies. Hugo and Lisa kissing on the front porch until his mother screamed at them to quit.

"My gosh," Daniel whispered. "Hugo. I haven't thought about him in years."

Meghan's face tightened to a scrunched, red ball. "How long were they together?"

Daniel stuttered, trying to remember. "They must have gotten together when I was ten or eleven," he said, not wanting to lie. "They were thirteen or fourteen."

Meghan let out a single, short wail, which she swallowed. "And do you know when they broke up?"

Daniel puffed out his cheeks. "Gosh, I don't know, Meghan." He certainly hadn't expected this.

"Try to remember," Meghan begged. "Please."

"They moved in together when they were eighteen," Daniel continued slowly. "They lived in an apartment on the outskirts of town because they couldn't afford anything much. If I remember right, Hugo got a job at a coffee shop, and Lisa worked at the flower shop. It's the same spot Claire Montgomery owns now."

Meghan hiccupped.

"I went over there a lot," Daniel admitted, "because Mom was really a piece of work by then, to the point that she accused me of doing everything wrong and ridiculed my every move. Made me feel like complete garbage. She thought Hugo was the only thing Lisa had ever done right — which meant she frequently called to ridicule her, too, even though she was out of the house. Hugo was really kind to me, always giving me a beer on the front porch and asking me how I was doing. He stepped in when Mom went over the line a few times, which I appreciated. But gosh, Hugo and Lisa fought."

Meghan's eyes sparkled with intrigue.

"I didn't have the best relationship with my sister," Daniel went on, "so every time they had an argument, I wasn't surprised. Although Hugo was just about the nicest guy in the world, Lisa was difficult to get along with. She was just like my mother used to be. You couldn't win with her. She boxed you into a corner during every argument. I sometimes felt terrible for Hugo as he fought to make it work between them. He knew her better than anyone, and she still cut him out sometimes."

"But you don't remember any of these arguments resulting in a breakup?" Meghan asked quietly.

"Sometimes Lisa spent the night at home," Daniel remembered. "She usually cried the entire time. Usually, Hugo would come pick her up in the morning, and they would make up. I really thought they were headed toward marriage. I mean, they'd been together forever. And they got engaged when they were sixteen or something, which is crazy to think about now. Maybe it was more typical back then."

Meghan looked mystified. She pressed her lips together, then removed her phone from her purse and pulled up several photographs she'd taken of Lisa's letters to Hugo. "I found these in the attic. They talk about a big breakup and insinuate that Hugo didn't want to see her again. In the letters, she's begging to get back together. They aren't dated, but you can sort of tell which one is the final letter. She's at the end of her rope, begging— telling him that all she's ever wanted is him."

Daniel was very quiet as he scanned through the photographs. His fingers itched to hold the letters in his hands, to read his sister's actual handwriting up close. It had been so long since he'd seen anything that belonged to her. It felt as though he was communicating with a ghost.

"I have this horrible theory," Meghan said, her voice harsh. "What if one of Hugo and Lisa's fights ended badly? What if they met back up again after one of these letters, got into another horrible argument, and something happened?"

Daniel jolted back, his chest shivering with surprise. Never in his wildest dreams had he considered this.

"Did you see Hugo after Lisa disappeared?" Meghan asked.

Daniel nodded, memories flicking through his mind's eye. "Once, I ran into him at the grocery store. He looked haggard like he'd been drinking too much. I asked him if he was all right since I knew Lisa had run off somewhere. He could barely look at me. It was like none of the memories we'd shared together had happened at all."

"What if he was guilty?" Meghan breathed. "What if he made her disappear? What if I'm one of those crazy women who don't know they're married to a murderer?"

Daniel gave her a look that echoed his doubt. "I know my sister," he told her. "And I think I know Hugo. It's much more likely that she ran off somewhere just to spite my mother, Hugo, and me."

Meghan's face fell as she nodded, sniffing.

"Why don't you ask Hugo about this?" Daniel coaxed.

"He was there. He knew her better than anyone. He's the only one who knows the whole story."

"What if I don't like his answer?" Meghan asked.

Daniel sighed. "I don't think it's going to be a nice story, no matter what. But I would bet my right hand on Hugo not having anything to do with Lisa's disappearance. He was— and presumably is— too good of a guy. You wouldn't have married him otherwise, would you have?"

Meghan hiccupped again, her face marred with doubt. "The past couple of weeks have made me question everything I've known about my marriage and about myself."

"I think that's what it means to be alive," Daniel managed. "Every day brings more questions."

"Do we have to answer every single one?" Meghan asked, trying to smile.

Out front came the sound of the bell, the one Daniel kept on the front counter just in case he was doing inventory when someone needed to check out. Daniel stood up just as an older woman out front hissed, "Debbie! Shush!"

Daniel froze, feeling as though his soul was rising out of his body. Meghan winced and clapped her hand over her mouth. His finger raised, Daniel walked from the backroom to find— horribly— that all seven of the women in the local Oak Bluffs book club were standing there expectantly. All between the ages of late-fifties and early eighties, they were the island's most successful gossip group. And based on the look in their eyes, they'd heard the majority of what Daniel and Meghan had been discussing.

Immediately, they burst apart like a flock of birds,

pretending as though they'd been studying the book-shelves, shopping the hours away. Daniel crossed his arms over his chest, trying to think of something to say that would stop them from telling everyone they knew about this. How had they snuck in without him hearing the front door, anyway? Ah. He noticed, now, that the bell he normally kept on the front door had fallen and was now strung outside across the porch.

"Can I get you ladies anything?" Daniel asked, his gut twisting.

"We're just browsing!" one of them called, her eyes glinting. She'd already gotten everything she'd come for.

Meghan appeared behind the counter, her face a pale shade of green. They locked eyes for a moment, both at a loss.

"Just talk to him," Daniel said under his breath. "Don't jump to any conclusions. He's a good man." Even as he said it, his stomach twisted even more, and he felt even more doomed to live a life alone.

But he remembered it clear as day: Hugo was a good man. It still had to be true, even all these years later. People didn't change so drastically. Lisa and his mother certainly never had.

Chapter Fifteen

In the parking lot of the grocery store, Meghan pulled her phone from her purse, bit her tongue, and typed in the family group chat:

> MOM: I want to call a family meeting.

> MOM: Tonight, at six.

Initially, she wrote she would bring Eva's favorite snacks and Theo's favorite beer, as she might have if they were just hanging out together to watch a film— but she hurriedly deleted both sentences, angry with herself for being so soft. She just loved them so much. It was hard to force herself to be so cold.

Meghan locked her car and headed into the grocery store with her head ducked low against the howling wind. The grocery store doors whipped open automatically and welcomed her into the warmth, where she grabbed a cart and set her stride toward produce. How many thousands of times had she gone grocery shopping? She hoped it would center her, that it would remind her of all the other normal years of her life.

But as she paused in front of the apples, which gleamed beneath the soft light, a few with purple bruises, she heard someone say her name. Meghan ducked around, searching the aisles behind her. Strangely, she was the only person in the produce section. She must have been hearing things.

But as she placed a bag of apples at the bottom of her cart and turned around, she heard it again— this time coming from one or two aisles over, perhaps where the chips or canned beans were kept. Meghan froze, listening intently. Overhead, classical music purred from the speakers, but it wasn't loud enough to keep her from hearing the gossip.

"That's right. Daniel Bloom and Meghan Coleman came out of the back of the bookstore— that Whale one we go to for our book club. You should have seen her face!" The woman's voice was on the older side, cracking with excitement.

A younger woman spoke quietly. "Are they having an affair?"

"It certainly looked like they were in cahoots," the older woman whispered. "But that's not all."

"You've really got the gossip today, don't you, Marge?" another woman laughed.

Meghan could imagine them two aisles away, their grocery carts parked in a circle as this little old woman named Marge spread the seeds of this horrific gossip. Meghan's heart pounded.

"They were talking about Hugo, Meghan's husband," Marge went on. "Now, I can't believe I forgot about this.

You remember who Hugo's girlfriend was before he started running around with the Coleman girl, don't you?"

"Oh, gosh. They were just a little bit younger than me," another woman said. "Who was that? I can picture her face!"

"It was Lisa Bloom, the bookstore owner's sister!" Marge announced proudly as though she'd cracked the code. "Hugo and Lisa were two peas in a pod. You never saw one without the other— that is, until approximately 1995 or 1996? I don't remember Hugo taking much of a break between Lisa and Meghan! One minute, he was basically married to the Bloom girl, and the next, I saw him eating pancakes with the Coleman girl!"

"Well, that's not so strange, is it?" another woman asked. "Young people move fast, and the Bloom women were always difficult. I remember hearing Lisa scream at Hugo in his pickup truck. I was terrified for him."

"The apple didn't fall far from the tree in Lisa's case," another said ominously.

"Although it's terrible what happened to Pam."

Everyone murmured in agreement, thinking of Pamela, Daniel's mother, sick with dementia.

Meghan's heart skipped several beats, bouncing around her chest as though it had forgotten how to keep her alive. The tips of her fingers were frigid with cold.

Marge lowered her voice to drop her final bomb, clearly thrilled she'd been allowed this morsel of gossip. It would boost her social standing for the foreseeable future.

"According to what me and the girls heard down at the bookstore, Meghan only just learned about Lisa.

According to Daniel, Lisa disappeared all those years ago," Marge continued. "And Meghan thinks Hugo had something to do with it."

Meghan felt as though she'd been punched. Abandoning her grocery cart, she walked around the corner, prepared to tell these gossips just what she thought about them. But just before she turned the corner to face them in the aisle, she stopped short, listening as Marge called another older woman over.

"You won't believe what we just learned about Hugo Porter today!"

Meghan closed her eyes, her hands in fists. As Marge recounted the story yet again, finishing with the suspicion that Hugo was, at best, a kidnapper and, at worst, a murderer, Meghan tried to come up with a plan. But if she leaped out and yelled at them right now, that wouldn't help her case in the slightest. Marge would just add to the gossip pile, telling everyone that Meghan was "delusional" and unwilling to face the truth about her husband. *"You should have seen how crazy she looked at the store!"* she imagined Marge saying at the coffee shop after this. *"I'm sure it's only a matter of time before Hugo is taken away and Meghan is in one of those Netflix documentaries."*

"Marge! What's this I hear about Hugo Porter being a murderer?" One of the cashiers called, abandoning her post and ambling toward the gossiping group.

Meghan groaned and fled, leaving her cart next to the apples and ducking back into the cold. Once in the driver's seat, she started the engine and pressed on the gas, ready to get out of there. But it was only two-thirty in the afternoon, and the family meeting wasn't planned for another three and a half hours. She felt she couldn't go home. Not yet. But as she drove across the island, her eyes filling with tears, she imagined the gossip she'd started spreading like wildfire, passing from cell phone to landline to next-door neighbor. "Hugo? Hugo Porter?" "You know, I always did wonder what happened to that Bloom girl." "You really can't trust anyone these days, can you?"

Back in June, the same hotel where Meghan and Hugo had had their first "unofficial" date had reopened after several years of refurbishment. Meghan was drawn there, burning rubber, until she parked in the lot surrounding the gorgeous, five-star boutique mansion, with its rolling green hills, its rocky cliffside, its croquet and tennis courts, and its pool, closed for the season. If she squinted hard, she could just barely remember the dilapidated mansion it had once been, the hotel where Hugo had pressed her up against the door frame and kissed her with a passion she'd never known. Now, she wondered if that passion had been a result of his recent breakup with Lisa. He'd been so angry, so lonely, coming off of an eleven-year relationship with a woman he'd wanted to marry. Had Meghan just been the next girl in line?

Meghan had never been inside the newly refurbished Aquinnah Cliffside. Before she entered, she checked her phone to find her children agreeing to the family meeting, plus a message from Daniel.

> DANIEL: A little old woman just came in here asking me about my sister's disappearance.

> DANIEL: I think we might be in over our heads.

Meghan turned off her phone, ready to block out the

world, and entered the beautiful hotel, pausing at the entryway to gaze up at the ballroom ceiling. Twenty-seven years ago, it had been rotting, with holes that birds and wind and rain had widened. She and Hugo had been able to see the old-world painting across the ceiling, just enough to feel mystified by another generation's appreciation for beauty. Now, as she walked slowly toward the ballroom, her heart filled her throat. Kelli Montgomery, the woman in charge of the redesign, had paid attention to every detail — including hiring someone to paint an exact replica of the mural on the ceiling. Meghan felt transported through time, both back to that black night in 1996 and further back to the forties when the hotel had been in full swing.

Meghan spent several hours in the dining room of the hotel, in awe of the ceiling above her, sipping tea and nibbling at a cheesecake. With her phone off, she knew nobody would find her— not at such an exclusive hotel, and gossip didn't reach these corners of the island, either. As a game, Meghan imagined she actually was Lisa Bloom, that she'd fled the island at the age of twenty-five and forged a new life elsewhere. She imagined she was the wife of a farmer in Ohio, that she was an airline stewardess flying over the Atlantic, and that she was a college professor discussing *The Great Gatsby* with a group of students.

Meghan hated how much space in her mind she'd given Lisa. It had been nearly impossible to think about anything else. And with the family meeting approaching, she was ready to clear the air.

Meghan drove back home, practicing what she wanted to say to Hugo in a low voice. When she arrived, Eva and Theo's cars were parked in the driveway, and she parked behind Eva's, unable to get into the garage. But when Meghan reached the front door, her key poised in front of the lock, she heard Hugo's voice, ragged and louder than ever. He was screaming.

"I don't know what to tell you! Lisa left! She disappeared! Why would I have had anything to do with it?"

Meghan winced, and her hand shook so hard that she couldn't find the keyhole.

"You people need to stop calling here!" Hugo cried. "Lisa broke my heart, you hear me? But I didn't hurt her! I'm not that kind of man!"

Meghan finally found the keyhole, and she shoved the key into it and twisted the doorknob. At the sound of the door, Eva flung herself into the foyer, her eyes red and blotchy. "Mom!" She hurried forward and wrapped her arms around Meghan, shaking. In the next room, Hugo ranted, maybe to Theo.

"The phone hasn't quit ringing," Eva breathed. "Everyone thinks Dad did something horrible." As she pulled back and gazed at her mother, she whispered, "Did he? Did he do this?"

Hugo's footfalls were violent, making the entire house shake. He appeared in the foyer behind Eva, his hair disheveled and his eyes buggy. He certainly looked the part of a murderer in a Netflix special. He opened his mouth, prepared to howl. But before he could, Meghan raised her palm to stop him.

"Me first," Meghan said firmly.

Feeling like the proud matriarch she was and had always been, Meghan led Eva, Hugo, and Theo into the living room, where she sat in her favorite chair, folded her ankles, and watched as the three people she loved the most in the world gathered across from her, pale-faced and shocked.

"I found your letters from Lisa Bloom," Meghan announced, her chin raised.

At hearing Meghan say the name of his ex-fiancé, his ghost, Hugo dropped his face into his hands.

"I didn't know what to think at first," Meghan continued. "I felt like a fool, of course. I thought we'd come together as two honest individuals, ready for a loving relationship and marriage. I couldn't stop playing over the events of our early relationship and how quickly we'd gotten together. I realized I'd been a replacement for this woman. A woman I'd never even heard of before!"

Hugo furrowed his brow and shook his head. "No. It was never like that, Meghan."

Meghan gave him a look that meant it wasn't time for him to speak yet. "Not long after that, I discovered that both Eva and Theo knew about Lisa, too. They'd been keeping it from me for eight years. For eight years, I'd been living in a house with people who didn't respect me enough to tell me the truth." Meghan swallowed the lump in her throat and forced herself to look Hugo in the eye. "What you and Lisa shared was so enormous. So all-encompassing. In reading her letters, I felt I was looking through a window at a version of you I was never allowed to know. And that hurt so much, Hugo."

Hugo was quiet for a long time. Bit by bit, the madness from his face faded, replaced with sorrow and contemplation.

"Can I tell you what it was like from my perspective?" Hugo asked.

Meghan nodded, trying to guard her heart from pain.

She knew it was futile, that this would hurt no matter what.

"I met you about a month after Lisa disappeared," Hugo said. "My friends had dragged me to that beach party to try to get my mind off of her. We'd already broken up about a dozen times at that point, and I was pretty sure Lisa was just hiding out somewhere, on the brink of sending me another letter or begging to get back together. To be honest with you, I missed her, but I was also so confused. I knew what we had was poisonous. And I had a feeling there was another kind of love out there. One that didn't feel like a prison."

On the kitchen wall, the house phone blared. Hugo's face transformed, and he leaped to his feet to answer it, disappearing behind the separating wall.

"Don't answer it, Dad!" Eva begged. "It's just more gossip. More people who don't know you."

Meghan heard Hugo stop walking and sigh. After a long pause, during which the phone rang and rang and finally finished, he reappeared in the doorway, looking like a damaged man. He stared at Meghan, his eyes lined with red.

"Meghan, you've known me so many, many years longer than Lisa knew me," Hugo breathed. "We've raised two wonderful children together. We've created this life. Do you honestly think I'm capable of hurting Lisa?"

Meghan dropped his gaze, her heart thrumming. Already, she felt so guilty for allowing those thoughts to rise up in her last night. It was her fault the gossip train had left the station. And it was going so quickly now; it was impossible to stop.

Meghan stood up and walked toward Hugo, sensing, for the first time in weeks, that they were finally seeing one another for who they were. November winds howled against the house and thrust the trees sideways, their branches flailing.

"I know you feel betrayed," Hugo said quietly. "But I want to do everything I can to remind you of how much I love you. I won't quit until you feel it."

Chapter Sixteen

D aniel returned home at seven-thirty that evening to find Caitlin, Aiden, and his mother around the dinner table. The sight was so alarmingly domestic, like something out of a 1950s' magazine, that it stopped Daniel in his tracks. Never had this house been a sight of love and companionship. Never had he seen so many people getting along at once.

"Hi, Dad." Caitlin stood to retrieve what she'd apparently spent the evening cooking— lasagna, which she now carried to the table to serve. "There's some wine. Would you like some?"

"This is amazing, Caitlin." Daniel watched as she slid a thick, cheesy, meaty slice of lasagna onto his plate, wondering the last time he'd eaten something so nourishing and coming up blank. Caitlin poured them both glasses of red wine, water for her grandmother, and water for Aiden. She worked quickly and diligently, as though she cared for them all the time. Daniel wondered what had gotten into her, but he didn't want to pry.

"We've had a few phone calls," Caitlin said as she

settled into the chair across from Daniel, cutting Aiden's lasagna.

Daniel winced. "Are they about your aunt?" He didn't want to say Lisa's name, as he knew it would kick-start his mother's anxiety. Right now, Pamela ate happily, her eyes dreamy.

Caitlin nodded. "They're saying crazy stuff."

"People need gossip to survive," Daniel said. "It's a misunderstanding."

"It is strange, though," Caitlin went on. "I mean, people don't really disappear anymore."

Daniel raised his shoulders. "She wanted to."

"And you're sure there wasn't foul play?"

Daniel sipped his wine, rolling the oaky flavor across his tongue. "I can tell you more after Aiden's bath, okay?"

Caitlin nodded, helping Aiden pick up his plastic fork. Daniel was reminded of doing the same for Caitlin, how proud he and Gina had been when Caitlin had figured out how to do basic things.

"It's delicious, Lisa," his mother announced firmly.

Caitlin's eyes widened. "Thank you, Mom?" she answered, raising her shoulders.

Satisfied, Pam continued to eat, chewing slowly, until she scraped her plate clean. It was more than Daniel had seen her eat in many months— nutrition she so needed, given how thin she'd gotten.

After they helped both Pam and Aiden with their bedtime rituals, Daniel and Caitlin gathered in the living room with a second glass of wine and spoke in quiet voices. Daniel explained that he'd recently befriended a woman named Meghan, who, as it turned out, was married to Lisa's longtime boyfriend, Hugo.

"What a strange coincidence," Caitlin breathed.

"Coincidences are more frequent on an island as small as this one," Daniel repeated. "But Meghan's been driving herself crazy, asking herself why her husband never told her about this enormous part of his past. And she asked herself all sorts of questions, including...."

"Whether or not her husband had something to do with Aunt Lisa's disappearance," Caitlin finished.

"Right. And she just happened to ask that out loud at the bookstore as eight women from the local book club listened on the other side of the wall," Daniel said.

Caitlin puffed out her cheeks. "Wow. That's bad."

"I haven't heard from Meghan yet," Daniel explained.

"I hope she's okay," Caitlin whispered.

Daniel gazed out onto the front porch, his head thick with memories. "I must have been twenty-one or twenty-two, and Hugo and Lisa were coming over for dinner. Mom made a mistake in the kitchen. I can't remember what it was, exactly— maybe she'd burnt the chicken pot pie. Who knows? Anyway, she was in a foul mood when they arrived. Almost immediately, she demanded Lisa come into the kitchen, where she began to ridicule everything about her. She said her clothes were inappropriate. She demanded why she wasn't married yet. She asked why she was so useless. I mean, it went on and on.

"Hugo and I were in here," Daniel went on, "drinking beers and listening to the entire thing. I was sort of embarrassed, but I also knew Hugo had heard it all before. By then, he and Lisa had already been dating for ten years. I tried to apologize to him, and he said something like, 'I get it, man. Families are weird.' But after they left that night, I sat in here, listening to Hugo and Lisa scream at each other. The fight started on the front porch and traveled across the driveway into their car. I heard Lisa calling Hugo every terrible name under the sun. I heard Lisa sobbing, telling Hugo he'd ruined her life. And I heard Hugo completely lose it. He told her that he wouldn't hesitate to leave her. That he was tired of her abuse. That he couldn't breathe anymore."

Daniel blinked back tears as the memories folded over him. He hadn't thought about that night in years.

Caitlin furrowed her brow. "Don't you think that's proof Hugo had something to do with Lisa's disappearance?"

"No. He just sounded like a man who needed out," Daniel said. "And now, the past is coming back to bite him. The island will not let him rest until it's proven that he had nothing to do with this. It's a mess." He sighed and glanced toward the darkened stairwell. "And that mess began with my mother, who alienated her children and taught them how to be cruel."

Caitlin was quiet for a moment, her dark eyes flickering with the light from the lamp on the end table.

And then, she said something that Daniel wanted to remember forever.

"You were never like that with me. I can't remember a single time you raised your voice, not to me or Mom."

Daniel's eyes immediately filled with tears. "I never wanted to be like them."

"And you aren't," Caitlin insisted, rolling her shoulders back. After another pause, she said, "I'm sorry I sided with Mom after she left. We were always so close, and I wanted to support her. And you were all the way over here, so far from where you'd raised me. I didn't know what to make of it. Plus, I was so hurt you were getting divorced. I know that's silly. I'm in my twenties. It's not like I can only live with you every other weekend or whatever. I'm not a child of divorce."

"It still feels debilitating when love falls apart," Daniel said quietly. "Especially when it's your parents' love."

He wasn't speaking for himself, of course. He'd barely known his father before he'd abandoned them. He'd never known a love he could believe in besides the one he'd had with Gina. He supposed that was why he clung to it so hard.

Caitlin stood up and walked across the living room, where she knelt to hug her father. Daniel felt exposed, as though his daughter now fully understood just how broken her father was. But maybe it was better to get everything out in the open. Maybe, instead of preaching what he felt about honesty, it was better to live it.

Chapter Seventeen

Sometime that night, snow spun from the thick clouds overhead and smothered them with a thick blanket of white. Meghan awoke in the guest bedroom, her eyes blinded by the light reflecting against the snow, and she hurried to peer out the window at what had to be a foot, at least. For a moment, she allowed herself the excitement she might have felt as a child. And then, she remembered she was in the midst of a tumultuous argument with her husband, half the island thought Hugo was a murderer, and her children were devastated at their parents' crumbling relationship.

As Meghan crept downstairs for coffee, a thick draft of cold air pressed against her face, and she cried out at the sight. Last night, a large tree limb had broken from the oak out front and busted through the bay window. It had snowed inside, piling up atop the cushions of the couch and layering atop the piano bench. The branch was too heavy for her to move by herself; Theo and Eva had both returned home last night before the snow had gotten too bad, which meant Meghan had only one person for help.

Meghan felt foolish, knocking on her own bedroom door. "Hugo?" She hadn't slept there since the first week of November, and she didn't want to overstep.

Hugo appeared in the crack of the door, rubbing one of his eyes groggily. "What's wrong?"

Meghan led Hugo to the staircase, where he could see the tree limb in all its busted glory. Immediately, he set his jaw, ready to craft a plan.

"We're going to need coffee," he said, reaching for his coat in the front closet and dropping his feet into his snow boots. "I'll get the branch moved."

"And I'll sweep up the glass," Meghan said.

For a brief second, they locked eyes, both noting how easy it was to become partners again. They'd done it seamlessly for decades.

As the piping hot coffee filled the pot, Meghan donned her own coat, fetched the broom and a pair of shoes, and set to work clearing the glass on the hardwood floor in the front room. Hugo had already hauled the large branch from the window and laid it across the snow. Eventually, Hugo would bring it to the backyard to dry out so he could chop it for firewood. Through the window, Hugo held up his left hand, which was stained red with blood.

"What did you do!" Meghan's heart seized with worry.

"I ticked myself on a piece of glass," Hugo explained nervously.

"Oh no." Meghan abandoned her broom and hurried back to the front door, beckoning for him to enter. "Let's get you cleaned up."

"We need to close the window," Hugo insisted.

"It's not supposed to snow anymore today," Meghan said. "We have time."

In their shared bathroom upstairs, Hugo sat on the toilet as Meghan scuffled through the cabinets, looking for a bandage for his inch-long cut. Although it was still bleeding, it looked clean and not too deep, requiring no hospital visit.

As Meghan dropped to her knees in front of her husband, she remembered perhaps hundreds of other incidents like this— with either Hugo or Meghan hurt or one of their children crying at the blood that seeped from their knees or fingers. Being in a family meant loving someone so much that their pain felt like your pain.

Meghan secured the bandage, her eyes filling with tears. It had been a long time since she'd touched Hugo so tenderly, and it made her realize how much she'd missed him.

"Get back in bed," Meghan ordered, sniffing. "I'll go get coffee and breakfast."

Hugo obeyed, removing his pants and returning to bed in just his boxers and t-shirt. Meghan felt light and happy, whipping back down the stairs, past the wide-open gash in the front of the house, toward the kitchen. There, she toasted English muffins, slathered them with butter and cheese, filled a bowl with blueberries, and poured their coffee. She carried the feast on a breakfast tray, trying and failing to remember the last time they'd done this.

Meghan placed the tray on the bed as Hugo held her eyes, smiling. He looked wordless.

"What are you thinking about?" Meghan asked. Her heart still felt like an open wound, bleeding as much as the cut on Hugo's hand. But she knew, now, that they would find a way to heal it. They would bandage it up.

Hugo sniffed and sipped his coffee. "I was thinking about how unfair I've been. I should have told you everything."

Meghan crossed her legs beneath her, waiting. She tried to tell herself she was ready.

"Lisa and I met when we were kids," Hugo began. "It was one of those things. We dated from the minute we understood what it meant to be 'boyfriend, girlfriend.' And we were always voted 'best couple' at the end of every year."

"It sounds like you never questioned it," Meghan suggested, her voice wavering.

"Not when I was a teenager," Hugo admitted. "In the same breath, those years were poisonous. Lisa had a big temper, and I matched her when I had to. The thing is, her home life was complicated. Her mother was cruel and manipulative. She threatened Lisa at every turn. One day, when Lisa was sixteen, her mother smacked her so hard that her face bruised."

"Oh my gosh." Meghan just couldn't imagine a mother acting that way.

"I wanted to go over to Lisa's place and warn her mother not to treat her like that," Hugo said. "But Lisa begged me not to. She said it would only get worse for her at home, which I believe was true. It was around that time that I asked her to marry me. I wanted to save her from that house." Hugo's eyes glinted. "But it was too late."

"What do you mean?"

Hugo sipped his coffee contemplatively. "Her mother had already influenced her too much. She couldn't free herself from that mentality. We moved in together after high school graduation, and the fights got so much worse after that. The things she said to me nearly shattered me. Sometimes, I stayed over at my buddies' places just to get away from her. She always found me, sending me letters, begging me to come back. Sometimes, she stayed over at her mother's house and sent the letters to where we lived together. We always found a way to work things out until one afternoon."

Hugo was quiet, rubbing his temples. Meghan thought, abstractly, that it was impossible to ever know someone fully, no matter how much you loved them.

"Like I said, this was just a month before I met you at that beach party," Hugo continued. "Lisa and I had gone grocery shopping and gotten into some stupid argument. I can't remember what it was about, honestly. I wish I could because it would prove to you how dumb it was. Anyway, when we got home, she said something cruel, then I echoed her cruelty back, and then— she hit me, hard, first on the shoulder, then on the arm."

Meghan placed her hand over her mouth.

"I know," Hugo hurried to add. "It probably sounds dumb. She was just a little woman without any real muscle, so it's not like her hitting me hurt that badly. But something about it triggered me. I realized I didn't want this woman anywhere near me. I didn't want her to raise my children. And I knew I had to end things once and for all."

"That is completely reasonable," Meghan whispered.

Hugo raised his eyebrows. "It was one of the hardest things I've ever done. I packed up all my things, told the landlord I was ending the contract, and told Lisa to go back to her mother's or find another place. I had another apartment lined up, the same one I was in when I met you. I never wanted to go back to that place again. And it was in my name, so it was all up to me.

"Lisa lost her mind when I told her, of course. I think she knew this breakup was different since I was officially getting rid of our place," Hugo went on. "She begged and pleaded with me and dropped off letter after letter at the coffee shop where I was working. Eventually, I banned her from the coffee shop, but she still had friends drop off the letters."

Meghan's head spun. "I can't believe how strong you were in resisting that."

"I knew we were codependent," Hugo said. "And that the only way to get away from her was no contact. But that summer, a little bit after I met you, her mother called me at home and demanded to know if Lisa was there. I said no, that I hadn't seen Lisa in months. Her mother said a few choice words to me, then hung up."

"And nobody ever told you she'd disappeared?" Meghan asked.

"Everyone knew I didn't want to talk about Lisa anymore," Hugo said, tilting his head. "I'd met someone else by that point. I wanted to become a different kind of person. And you taught me how."

Meghan leaned back, her heart stirring with love for him. She'd never understood the depths of his love for her until now. To him, she'd fished him out of a devastating time of his life and helped him move forward. To her, he'd just been the cute guy at the beach party who'd taught her how to live.

"I shouldn't have kept those stupid letters," Hugo added quietly. "They were my last connection to that time of my life, a time I had to abruptly say goodbye to. My youth when I was young, wild, free, and very, very stupid. On the other hand, I didn't want you to know about that side of me. I feel like before I met you, I was a completely different person— one I'm not sure I like."

"I understand," Meghan whispered because, finally, she really did. Atop the comforter, she laced her fingers through Hugo's good hand, marveling at how much closer she felt to him now that everything was out in the open. From here, they could move forward, side-by-side, with a denser relationship. "I love you, you know."

"I love you. So much," Hugo breathed. "I couldn't believe how quickly I fell in love with you. It was like you were always waiting for me on the other side of my poisonous relationship. I wasn't sure I deserved you. Yet here you are, sitting on my bed all these years later. How lucky am I?"

Chapter Eighteen

D aniel's grandson had never seen a snowfall like this. All bundled up, cheeks shining, Aiden leaped through the backyard, cupping snow in his mittens and crying out to his mother about how beautiful it was. From the back porch, where he sipped his coffee next to Pam, Daniel nearly wept with joy. He wanted to remember this moment for the rest of his life.

Even Pam seemed thrilled with the snowfall. Daniel had helped her into winter garb— sweaters, Long Johns, extra socks, a thick coat, gloves, and a hat, laced up her snow boots, and led her outside, where her eyes had glinted at the winter wonderland. Now, as she gazed down at Aiden and Caitlin, she said, "Look at little Danny. He just loves the snow."

Daniel had to go inside for a moment to pull himself together. Every emotion felt too intense, threatening to drown him. He couldn't help but ask himself: once upon a time, had his mother actually loved him and Lisa the way he loved Caitlin? Had she always loved them and just been unable to show it? There weren't many photographs of Lisa and Daniel's childhood, no real proof that Pam had cared to document the passage of time. Still, she'd fed them. Still, she'd made sure they had clothes to wear and school supplies.

Some people just don't know how to show their love, he thought. And wasn't that a tragedy?

When Daniel came back outside, Pam was in the backyard with Aiden, pulling snow into a snowball that she whacked against a tree so that the snow exploded. This pleased Aiden, and he clapped and said, "Again!" Caitlin's eyes met Daniel's over the snow, and she smiled. Was this the healing his family had always needed?

After the chilly wind off the Vineyard Sound became too intense, Daniel gathered his family inside for hot cocoa and grilled cheese sandwiches. Caitlin put on *The Golden Girls*, which Aiden had come to like as well, and Pam and her great-grandson sat happily watching it, like two peas in a pod.

"I called Brent last night," Caitlin said softly, rolling up the sleeves of her wool sweater and leaning against the kitchen wall as Daniel flipped a grilled cheese in the skillet. The kitchen was filled with the smell of browning bread and warm butter.

"Oh?" Daniel didn't want to press her for any more information than she wanted to give.

"The conversation didn't go very well," Caitlin admitted. "But it's a start."

Daniel nodded. "I'm proud of you for trying."

"I heard a rumor that human relationships are all about forgiveness," Caitlin said with a laugh. "I'm trying to forgive myself along the way, too. That's proving to be the hardest one of all."

"It always is."

After they ate, their fingers slick with butter and their stomachs filled with melted cheese, Aiden and Pam went down for afternoon naps, and Caitlin set herself up in the living room with a book. Daniel remained in the kitchen, his heart thrumming. He knew what he needed to do, and for some reason, after all this time, he finally felt strong enough to do it.

Holding his breath, Daniel pulled up the divorce papers on his computer. He'd hardly glanced at them when they'd arrived in his inbox, choosing to ignore the problem as long as he could. Now, he scanned over the legal jargon that separated him from the only woman he'd ever loved. It seemed needlessly cruel. It also was exactly what she wanted— and he was ready to give it to her.

With a flourish of his finger on his touchpad, Daniel signed the divorce papers and emailed them to Gina's lawyer and Gina herself. He then checked the Sent folder to make sure it had gone out, half hoping there had been a mistake, that technology had swooped in to save his marriage. Unfortunately, the email had gone through, which meant it was over. He was a single man, and Gina was free.

Within the hour, he received a call from Gina— her first in nearly a year.

"Daniel. Hi." She sounded warm and slightly surprised. It reminded Daniel of when she'd sometimes called on her way home from work, asking if he wanted her to pick up a pizza— something so normal he hadn't thought to be grateful for. "Thank you for signing the papers."

Daniel leaned back in his chair and fluffed his hair. "Yeah. Thanks for your patience."

Gina laughed kindly, and Daniel stood up and went

out to the front porch, where he closed the door between himself and his daughter. He wasn't sure he wanted Caitlin to hear.

"Why the change of heart?" Gina asked.

"It's been an interesting November, to say the least. I've had a lot of time to think."

Gina was quiet for a moment. "How is our girl doing?"

"I think she's going to be okay," Daniel said. "To be honest, having her here has been..." He paused, trying to come up with the correct word for the tremendous love he felt. "I'm just happier than I've been in a long time."

"I'm really glad to hear that."

Daniel touched the glass that wrapped around the porch, and it was frigid on his fingertips. "Can I ask you a question?"

"Of course."

"Was I a terrible husband?"

"What! No." Gina laughed again. "Never."

Daniel furrowed his brow, swimming through memories he couldn't make sense of anymore. "I'm so sorry I dragged you out to Martha's Vineyard. I never should have done that."

"We both know that was just the final nail in the coffin," Gina said softly. "I came with you because I wanted to try to make it work, too. But it was just too far gone."

Daniel closed his eyes. This was exactly what he'd suspected. He wished they'd been able to find that language years ago if only to help them through the rocky journey from separation to divorce.

"It's really sad," Gina whispered. "It nearly killed me, too. But we owe it to ourselves to move on." After a long pause, she asked, "Are you actually happy out east? California was your home for so many years. I'm sorry if this is crass to ask, but why don't you put your mean old mother in a nursing home and leave?"

Daniel shook his head tentatively. "The Vineyard is my home again, for better or for worse." That, and because he wasn't like Lisa; he didn't just flee.

"Well, Caitlin has certainly fallen in love with that island," Gina said. "It must have some kind of magic I never understood."

"What has she told you?" Daniel asked.

"That Aiden loves his grandfather, which is no surprise to me," Gina said, her voice breaking. "And that her Grandma Pam doesn't know where or who she is, but that you're taking great care of her. You always had so much love to give, Daniel. Given who your family is, I don't know how you managed that. But I can only thank you for the love you showed me over the years. It truly changed my life."

After Daniel and Gina wished one another well and made loose plans to have coffee the next time Daniel came out to California, Daniel tip-toed back into the house to find Caitlin asleep, her book strewn across her lap, and her lips parted. Her eyes flickered behind their lids as though she rolled through dreamlands. He would have done anything to know what she dreamed about.

Daniel took a book to the lazy boy, shifting back and inhaling deeply. He felt as though, in the act of ending his twenty-six-year marriage, he'd run a marathon, as though he'd pushed his body to an inconceivable limit and now had to find a way to repair himself again. At fifty, there was still so much living left— decades of it if he was lucky. Maybe he would get back on the dating apps. Maybe he would find a way to take a woman to dinner and not feel as though he had three heads.

His phone buzzed with a text from Meghan, whom he hadn't heard from all day.

> MEGHAN: Hey there. How are you holding up after the snow?

> DANIEL: It was a nice day. My grandson had never played in the snow before.

> MEGHAN: That must have been magical.

> MEGHAN: I wanted to say...

> MEGHAN: Thank you for reminding me my husband is a good man. I knew, in my heart of hearts, that he never would have hurt someone.

> MEGHAN: My sense of betrayal got the better of me. I turned into a monster for a little while.

> MEGHAN: You were the only thing keeping me on solid ground.

> MEGHAN: Thank you for that.

> DANIEL: I hate that the ghost of my sister came up from the past to hurt more people. I guess I shouldn't be surprised, though. She had a knack for that.

> DANIEL: Hugo is so lucky he met someone like you after the drama of that relationship. If anyone can get through this, you can.

> DANIEL: By the way, I finally signed the papers.

MEGHAN: YOU DID?

MEGHAN: Oh my gosh. We have to celebrate as soon as the snow clears.

MEGHAN: This is the first day of the rest of your life. It's going to be fantastic. Trust me.

DANIEL: I know you're right.

DANIEL: And I'm ready for it. Bring it on.

Chapter Nineteen

T he following morning, Oak Bluffs road officials cleared the snow enough for business to resume as usual. Daniel bustled around the kitchen, surprised at how light he felt after signing the divorce papers, as though a burden had been lifted. He made oatmeal for his mother, who was quiet but smiling to herself, and listened to Aiden tell them a story he'd made up about his stuffed animal. Caitlin appeared soon after, recently showered, and said Cindy had just texted to say she couldn't make it to watch Pam today.

"You have Cindy's number?" Daniel's eyebrows rose.

"We exchanged last week," Caitlin explained easily.

Daniel frowned into his own oatmeal, weighing up how to tackle the day.

"Don't worry, Dad," Caitlin assured him, reading his mind. "Aiden and I don't have anywhere to go today. We'll be here with Grandma." She smiled serenely at Pam.

Daniel was touched. Stuttering, he thanked Caitlin, promising to bring home fried chicken for dinner that night. Caitlin assured him it was no problem, that there was nothing more she liked than cozying up in that house with Aiden, playing games and reading. "I'm a California girl," she said, "but I've fallen in love with the cold."

Daniel drove to the post office to pick up several boxes of books, which hadn't been delivered directly to the bookstore for a reason that wasn't clear to him. Maybe he had to sign something. He parked in the back lot and walked through the sharp chill along the sidewalks coated with salt. Downtown was decorated for Christmas already, with wreaths adorning several small business doors and garlands wrapped around trees. It wasn't long until Thanksgiving, and Daniel dared to dream Caitlin and Aiden would stay for it. Perhaps he and Caitlin could alternate cooking tasks. He imagined them laughing at the amount of leftovers, their bellies stuffed.

There was a short line at the post office, and Daniel waited happily, listening as people he vaguely recognized greeted the postal woman and asked how she'd handled the snow.

"I was grateful for a day off!" she said each time, as though she never grew tired of having the same conversations over and over again.

Daniel retrieved three boxes of books, each heavier than the last, and piled them by the door, weighing up how to transport them to his vehicle. Just before he headed out with the first box, the bell above the door jangled, announcing the arrival of Ben Walsh, a man Daniel would have recognized anywhere.

"Daniel?" Ben's smile widened. "Daniel Bloom?"

"Hey, Ben." Daniel grimaced. Back in high school, Ben had been one year younger than Lisa and two years older than Daniel. Although Lisa had always dated Hugo,

Ben had never tired of chasing after her, demanding her attention. He'd been very sure that his intellect and good looks would eventually lure Lisa away from Hugo. It obviously hadn't worked.

Now, Ben's eyes stirred with intrigue. "I've been meaning to call you. This news about Lisa has really broken me up inside."

Daniel tried his best not to roll his eyes. Ben was always melodramatic, all in an attempt to get what he wanted.

"Do you really think Hugo had something to do with her disappearance?" Ben asked. "I never trusted how quickly he moved on after she was gone. It was like he planned it."

"Hugo is a good man," Daniel said firmly, lifting up the box of books, hoping Ben would get the hint he didn't want to chat.

"But don't you wonder what happened to her?" Ben demanded, stepping in front of Daniel. "I mean, nobody knows. Not you. Not your mother. Not even me. Your sister and I were good friends. It just seems strange she never reached out."

Daniel sighed and set down the box of books again. "Lisa left, and she didn't want to be found. That sums it up, don't you think?"

But Ben wasn't finished. "A few of us have formed a search party. We're doing everything we can to get to the bottom of what happened. And we haven't ruled Hugo out yet."

"Beg your pardon?" Daniel could hardly believe his ears.

"I just hope we don't discover something truly tragic," Ben went on before lowering his voice. "But don't you think it'll be nice to finally know where she is? You're not the only one who lost her, you know. We did, too."

As he filled his trunk with boxes of books, Daniel's head stirred with annoyance. For years, he'd pushed the "what happened to Lisa" question to the very far corners of his mind, set on building his own life without her. With Ben poking and prodding at these questions, however, Daniel was reminded just how much her disappearance bothered him. Of course, he'd feared for her safety. Of course, a part of him had always wondered if something had gone wrong.

A few minutes after Daniel opened the bookstore for the morning, Meghan appeared in the doorway, all bundled up, her blonde highlights bursting from beneath a thick red winter's hat.

"Morning!"

Daniel hovered over one of his new boxes of books and smiled. "This is a surprise."

"I had to run some errands," Meghan explained, peering down at his new books and nodding with approval. "Plus, I finished the Zevin book and need something else."

Daniel rubbed his palms together, grateful to think about his favorite topic— recommending books to the dearest people in his life. "The new Ann Patchett is supposed to be incredible," he explained, striding toward the fiction section to find *Tom Lake*. "I haven't gotten to it yet. Tell me how it is?"

Meghan took the book without bothering to read the blurb on the back, putting her trust in him completely. "The Zevin was so good. I cried throughout the entire last third."

"Me too," Daniel assured her. "I still wake up thinking about it."

They shared a soft smile, both lost in a fictional world for a blissful moment.

And then, Daniel remembered. "There's a search party looking for my sister."

"Really?" Meghan's eyes stirred with panic. "Have they found anything?"

"Not yet. To be honest, it's helmed by this guy who was obsessed with her back in high school. I can only assume his reason for looking for her is questionable, at best."

"I just hope they know what they're doing," Meghan breathed.

Daniel placed several books on the shelf in front of him. "We don't need her. She can stay wherever she is." His voice wavered, proof that he wasn't entirely sure of that.

"So many years have passed," Meghan said. "Maybe things are different."

"Lisa would need an entire personality change for that to happen," Daniel insisted.

Meghan was quiet for a moment, her lips pressed together. "I just can't help but think of what you first told me," she said. "About the importance of honesty. About bringing the truth to the light. Maybe you deserve that truth from your sister, too."

Daniel sighed and slid more books onto the shelf. He suddenly felt very tired, as though he could sleep for ten years straight.

"Hugo told me more about your mother," Meghan said quietly. "About how cruel she was to you and Lisa."

She shook her head. "I can't believe you came all the way to Martha's Vineyard from California to take care of her."

"Loyalty might be my biggest flaw," Daniel said. "But regardless, my mother isn't the woman she once was. She's like a child in many ways. She just needs care. She needs companionship. And, maybe due to my loneliness, I can offer that in droves."

Meghan touched his shoulder tenderly. "Loyalty is never a flaw," she assured him. "You're a force for good in the world, Daniel. Please remember that. And know you're not alone anymore. I'm here. Your daughter is here. And we're going to support you."

Chapter Twenty

The following evening, normality continued to settle around the Porter Family, so much so that Meghan could almost pretend none of the previous couple of weeks had happened. Almost. Hugo had plans to watch a basketball game with a friend, which allowed Meghan to arrange to meet her children for dinner downtown. Things had been horribly strained between them. She needed to clear the air.

Eva and Theo drove together to the restaurant. Meghan watched as they got out of Theo's car and walked side-by-side toward the Mexican restaurant, their faces strained as they spoke in low tones. It was almost impossible to imagine what they said. Meghan stood up as they entered, smiling as they approached. She hated that she could hear the angry words she'd said to both of them echoing in her head. She wrapped them both in a hug, closing her eyes as the tension in her shoulders loosened.

"I'm so sorry I was so angry with you," she whispered above Eva's shoulder. "I know you just wanted to protect me."

In her embrace, Eva relaxed, and her voice was round and soft, almost like a song.

"We were stupid," Eva said.

"And we panicked," Theo assured her.

Meghan slid back into the booth and crossed her ankles. Eva and Theo sat across from her, touching their menus nervously.

"When I think about it rationally, I know I wouldn't have handled it well back then, either," Meghan said, tucking her hair behind her ears.

"Do you think you would have gotten divorced?" Eva whispered.

"Are you going to get divorced now?" Theo asked, his voice rising. He sounded much younger than his twenty-four years.

"Your father and I needed to talk about this at some point," Meghan said. "Maybe it all came out into the open at the right time. Or maybe there was never a right time! I don't know." She rubbed her temples, waving off a headache. "Your father was broken-hearted about his ex-fiancé when we met, and he didn't know how to talk about it. It's not like I would have known what to say, either. Maybe I wouldn't have wanted to date him. Maybe I would have used his ex as an excuse not to get close to him. I wasn't exactly into dating at the time. I was driven. My friends told me I wasn't living." Meghan's lips twisted at the memories.

"Why didn't Dad go to therapy?" Theo asked. "To help him through the breakup? That's what I would have done to move on."

Meghan laughed gently. "I love your generation's ease with talking about these things. Therapy just wasn't something people did back then. We bottled up our feelings and hoped for the best."

"That does not sound healthy," Eva said.

"And you see what resulted," Meghan offered. "It became a storm of anger and resentment. And it nearly destroyed all of us."

"Ugh." Eva rolled her shoulders forward and dropped her elbows on the table. "What else did Dad say about this woman?"

"Your father can tell you everything himself," Meghan said. "I don't want to speak for him. Suffice it to say, I understand where his heart is at right now. And I want to keep working to build a better and more honest relationship."

Theo and Eva exchanged glances, seeming to have a silent conversation over the table.

"You've always been the happiest couple I've ever known," Theo said finally. "It's why it was so easy to forget about the letters from Lisa eight years ago. We just shoved them in the attic and went back to our normal lives. If I remember correctly, when Eva and I got downstairs, you and Dad were sharing a bottle of wine and laughing your heads off over a movie. It made it almost impossible to think of the letters as legitimate."

"Seriously. Sometimes I wonder if Finn and I are as happy as you guys," Eva joked.

Meghan's heart swelled, and her mind's eye filled with thousands of gorgeous, sun-dappled images of her Hugo: sitting by her on the couch, at the dining room table, across the car, or next to her in bed, always a split-second away from sharing a joke with her or bubbling with laughter of his own.

"No matter how happy we are, we still need to work

at it," Meghan said softly. "Marriage is a challenge. Maybe, looking back, your father and I entered into it lightly. We loved each other. I was pregnant. We wanted to see what happened next together. And your father wanted to leave his demons behind."

"They always catch up to you," Theo said. "That's the plot of every horror movie, isn't it?"

Meghan laughed. "The past couple of weeks have been my own personal horror movie. I'm so glad they're over!"

A waiter arrived with three glasses of water filled with ice, a bag of tortilla chips, and a bowl of salsa. It had been ages since Meghan had eaten chips, and she filled each one with chunky tomato and onion and asked her children about their days, ready to speak about something besides the murky past, filled with mistakes. Now that the air had cleared, they laughed easier and spoke with their hands. According to Eva, Finn had a new love—CrossFit, and he wouldn't shut up about it. "You should see all the new protein powder he bought for the kitchen, Mom! It's disgusting." Theo had gone on another date a few nights ago, but it had ended terribly. "She has halitosis, Mom! I couldn't stand it!" Meghan howled with laughter.

The burritos were literally the size of their heads, stuffed with cheese, refried beans, beef, rice, and vegetables, and Meghan struggled to eat even half of hers, touching her stomach as she collapsed in her chair. Theo tucked his in easily as Eva looked at him, horrified.

"What?" Theo asked, dotting his napkin across his lips. "I'm a growing boy."

"You're twenty-four," Eva said, rolling her eyes. "With the metabolism of a child. I'm so jealous!"

"It's a life-long struggle," Meghan said. "Your father still eats like a horse."

The waiter came to drop off the bill, and Meghan slid it over to her side of the table before Theo or Eva could flinch. "Next time," she told them with a wave of her hand, although she knew she would scramble to pay for their dinners for as long as she could. Meghan snapped her credit card onto the table and raised her eyes just as a group of three middle-aged women in puffy coats burst into the restaurant, carrying flyers. A chilly draft rolled over the restaurant, refreshing after such an enormous meal.

"Evening, ladies." Their waiter approached with a hospitality smile. "Three tonight?"

"We just want to drop these off," the woman in the front said, raising the flyers. "We're looking for a missing person."

The waiter palmed the back of his neck and gestured vaguely toward the bulletin board near the hostess table. There, islanders had posted everything from "Help Wanted" to "Rooms Available" to "Pet Sitter Needed" signs. Meghan's heartbeat dully, as though she were deep underwater, as the leader of the search party tacked three flyers up on the bulletin board, taking up more than a quarter of the space. Each featured a photograph of Lisa Bloom from twenty-seven years ago. Her blonde hair was too bright for the printer they'd used, which made her head look grainy. Above the photograph was the word: MISSING, and below it was more information regarding where she'd last been seen, what she'd been wearing, and who to contact if you knew anything. Just before the women left the restaurant, they eyed Meghan, their cheeks slack. They looked at her as though she was the villain in the story, responsible for Lisa's disappearance.

As the women departed, set on putting their flyers all over town, Eva and Theo followed Meghan's gaze across the restaurant.

"Goodness," Eva breathed. "They're bent on finding her."

"I really don't think she wants to be found," Theo said. "She left for a reason."

"Maybe she changed her name," Eva suggested. "Maybe she moved to another country."

"Everything is possible," Meghan said, raising her shoulders.

"Gosh, it would be weird if she came back," Eva said. "Especially since you said Dad never really dealt with his heartbreak around it. Her coming back would mean he would have to, right?"

"I wonder what they would say to one another." Theo sipped the last of his Diet Coke, his eyes in slits.

Meghan shivered, trying to shove the images away. Dread filled her lungs. If Hugo ever saw Lisa again, would he remember something about himself, something he'd thought had died long ago? Would he find a piece of himself in her eyes, proof that he'd never really loved Meghan the way he was supposed to?

"I'm ready to get out of here." Meghan tried to smile and waved her credit card through the air to attract the waiter. "Thank you for a wonderful evening. I love you both."

Her children told her they loved her too, so much, but their voices hardly penetrated the worry that filled her ears.

Chapter Twenty-One

O n Thanksgiving morning, Daniel awoke at six and tip-toed to the kitchen. There, he stood in the shadows of the morning, watching the sun peek its head over the snow-capped rooftops of his neighborhood and stream through the skeletal limbs of trees. Coffee brewed in the pot, warm and nutty, and upstairs, his daughter, Aiden, and his mother continued to sleep, soft in their beds, their bellies empty and ready for a day of perpetual eating.

Just a month ago, Daniel had ached with fear for this holiday, worried he would spend it alone with his books as his mother watched television. Now, he had his work cut out for him.

Daniel had bought a turkey, along with ingredients for stuffing, mashed potatoes and gravy, Brussels sprouts, yams, and fresh rolls. Yesterday afternoon, he and Caitlin had baked three types of pie, apple, pecan, and pumpkin, playing music on the kitchen radio as they chatted about this and that. Throughout, Aiden had played with his plastic cars on the floor, making "vroom" noises with his lips.

Now, the pies waited expectantly on the counter, their sugar-filled dough shimmering, a sign of the love that filled this house.

Daniel hadn't asked Caitlin about Brent, about whether she'd been honest with him about her whereabouts or whether she'd considered returning home. He knew this was selfish on his part, that, privately, he wanted her and Aiden to stay forever. The knowledge that Brent was out there, missing them, sometimes kept Daniel awake at night. Then again, Daniel's own loneliness had kept him awake for what felt like years at this point. He told himself to enjoy this time for as long as it lasted.

The turkey needed four hours in the oven, just enough for them to eat by two that afternoon. As soon as it was in the oven, the house seemed to come alive around him, brimming with smells of sage, butter, and crackling white meat. A few minutes later came the sound of Aiden upstairs, babbling happily to his mother. Caitlin carried him downstairs, smiling sleepily.

"You've been up for a while!"

"I was too excited," Daniel said. "And the turkey wasn't going to baste itself."

Aiden reached out for his grandfather, and Daniel took him in his arms as Caitlin bubbled around the kitchen, pouring herself coffee. Aiden tugged at Daniel's ear gently as Daniel asked him how he'd slept, whether he'd had any dreams. Daniel had thought several times about recording their conversations, as it always seemed Aiden had something fantastical to say. That imagination always sloughed off at puberty. Why was that?

"What is Meghan doing today?" Caitlin asked, helping Aiden into the highchair at the table— a recent purchase that seemed to indicate they were sticking around for a while.

"She's at her sister's place," Daniel answered.

"Ah! Oriana. I saw her again the other day at the bookstore. She's really impressive. An art dealer?" Caitlin removed a big jar of applesauce from the fridge and portioned it into a bowl for Aiden to serve himself, which he always did with the air of a modern painter— flashing apple sauce all over his cheeks and bib.

"Meghan was just telling me a crazy story about her," Daniel went on as he stirred the stuffing with a big wooden spoon. "About how she sold a three-million-dollar painting at the beginning of her career, but it was just revealed to be a forgery."

Caitlin's eyes widened. "Is that a crime?"

Daniel raised his shoulders. "She didn't know it was a forgery at the time. She was going to come clean to the person she sold the painting to, but he died, unfortunately."

"Wow." Caitlin shook her head. "I can hardly imagine three million dollars, let alone spending three million on a painting."

"What would you spend three million dollars on?" Daniel asked, his voice light.

Caitlin tilted her head, her eyes upon her son as he scooped applesauce to his chin, missing his mouth. "I would buy one of those beautiful coastal houses here on the Vineyard, one big enough for you, Grandma, Aiden, and..." She trailed off, folding her lips. "And Brent, I guess. If he moved."

Daniel stopped stirring, surprised. "You would want to stay on the Vineyard?"

More, he wanted to ask: you would actually leave your mother behind in California? Wouldn't you regret that?

Caitlin's eyes glowed. "It's such a nice environment here, especially for children. And you know, with my work, I can live anywhere."

Daniel was vaguely aware of Caitlin's career as a copywriter, but it wasn't something she'd spoken about often.

"What would Brent think?"

"He knows we need a change," Caitlin said quietly. "And he's willing to come out here to try."

Daniel's heart nearly leaped out of his chest. "Tell him he's welcome any time!"

Caitlin's cheeks were blotchy as she turned to face him. "He's coming today, I think. By the afternoon."

"Wow!" Daniel staggered away from the counter, unsure if he should hug her or if this was even good news at all. Her face was difficult to read, a result of her fear. "How are you feeling about that?"

"I don't want to fight with him anymore," Caitlin breathed. "I told him everything that's happened here on Martha's Vineyard since I got here and that it's reminded me of the beauty of forgiveness and moving on. I want Brent to be in Aiden's life. But more than that, I want Brent and I to work on our relationship and to be honest with one another. I want us to build a wonderful and strong family."

"Brent?" Aiden raised his chin, showing off the thick applesauce across his lips and nose.

"That's right, buddy. Your daddy is coming," Caitlin

said, her voice breaking. "We're ready to see him, aren't we?"

Daniel wavered uneasily on his feet, his heart thumping. "Good thing we made three pies," he tried to joke. "We're going to need them."

As Caitlin cleaned Aiden's hands and face with a wet cloth, Pam cried out from the top floor. Daniel bolted up the staircase to find his mother in her nightgown, perched at the edge of her bed, gazing out the window.

"What's wrong, Mom?" Daniel was out of breath, his blood pressure spiking.

"I just saw the most beautiful bird at the window," Pam explained, folding her wrinkled hands over her thighs. "A cardinal. Oh, Lisa just loves cardinals. Tell her to come in here just in case it comes back."

Daniel helped his mother dress for the day, selecting a dark green sweater, a pair of slacks, and a thick pair of wool socks. Throughout, he spoke to her, hoping his narrative would draw her deeper into the world of memory. He told her about Brent coming from California and about his hopes that Caitlin would be able to rebuild her marriage. He told her about his divorce from Gina, about how it had broken his heart. He also told her about Meghan, about how kind she'd been to him during a dark era of his life. "It's rare to meet someone you click with so completely," he explained as he guided his mother toward the staircase.

"That's what I always say," Pam returned, giving him a nod of wisdom.

Downstairs, Caitlin kissed her grandmother on the cheek and guided her to her chair in the living room. "Happy Thanksgiving, Grandma!"

"It's Thanksgiving, is it?" Pam asked in disbelief.

"It is," Caitlin explained, "and Dad has made the most delicious feast. We're all going to sit down together and enjoy it later, okay?"

"That sounds mighty nice," Pam said, rocking back in her chair. "Lisa had better make her pumpkin pie."

Daniel returned to the kitchen counter and heaved a sigh. Caitlin squeezed his elbow gently and whispered, "Did Lisa actually make pumpkin pie?"

"There was one year she did," Daniel remembered. "She was living with Hugo at the time, and she brought a few pies over for Thanksgiving. If I remember correctly, one of them fell off the counter, and the pie pan shattered into a billion shards of glass. Mom had a really good time with that one, telling Lisa what an idiot she was."

Caitlin winced. "Gosh, I cannot imagine speaking to Aiden like that."

In the living room, Pam howled at something one of the Golden Girls said, rocking happily in her chair. Daniel told his heart to calm. His family's unhappiness remained locked in the past.

At twelve-thirty, Caitlin whirled through the kitchen, her face frantic as she thrust her arms through her coat sleeves. "Brent's ferry just got in."

Daniel's heart thudded as he dried his hands on a kitchen towel. "Should we all go?"

"I'd like to go alone," Caitlin answered, "if I can borrow your car?"

"I'll watch Aiden," Daniel assured her.

Caitlin reached the door and wrapped her hand around the knob, where she took a long, staggered breath.

"Just tell him how much you love him," Daniel urged her quietly. "In the end, that's all that matters in the world, doesn't it?"

Caitlin glanced his way as though she were surprised he'd recognized the pain etched on her face. "I love you, Dad."

"I love you so much, Bean."

With the food more-or-less ready, Daniel collapsed on the floor next to Aiden and filled the next anxious minutes playing with him. Although maybe it was a trick of his imagination, Aiden looked stronger and bigger than he had when they'd arrived, as though the chilly island weather had strengthened his bones. Daniel had a sudden instinct, and he grabbed his phone to take a photograph of Aiden with his cars, his tongue between his lips as he concentrated. He sent it to Gina, along with the text:

> DANIEL: This little guy is growing like a weed!

> DANIEL: Happy Thanksgiving.

> DANIEL: We miss you.

> GINA: There's my little guy! I love him so much.

> GINA: Thank you for sending that to me.

> GINA: I wish you all a wonderful Thanksgiving.

Just as his car appeared in the driveway, with Caitlin in the driver's seat and Brent in the passenger, Daniel placed an extra place on the dining room table and lined it with two differently sized forks and two knives. Had his mother not been sick, she might have shamed him for not putting them in the right place. But, he reasoned, that had never mattered. Not in the slightest.

Caitlin and Brent's happy voices bubbled through the

house as they entered. Daniel remained in the dining room for a moment, listening as Aiden rammed into his father's legs and greeted him joyously. "Daddy!" Caitlin laughed and spoke in whispers so that Daniel could just barely hear her say: "He missed his daddy so much. We both did." Daniel's heart shattered.

In a normal voice, Caitlin introduced Brent to her grandmother, saying, "Grandma, this is my husband, Brent. And Brent, this is Grandma Pam."

"Aren't you handsome," Pam suggested, a smile in her voice.

Daniel filled his lungs, trying to combat his nerves, and headed to the living room, bent on shaking Brent's hand. When he entered, Brent turned and smiled nervously, a six-foot-three, muscular man whose heart had just gone through the wringer. Daniel knew better than most that it took a different sort of power to accept someone's apology.

"Good to see you again, Brent," Daniel said. "It's been a long time."

"Too long," Brent said. "You have a gorgeous island out here. As a west coaster, I never could have imagined."

Daniel laughed and locked eyes with Caitlin, who looked on the verge of floating out the window, such was the joy that echoed from her eyes.

"It's our own little oasis," he said. "I hope you're not too cold."

"Not in the slightest." Brent lifted Aiden into his arms and tossed him into the air so that Aiden shook with giggles.

"I hope you're hungry," Daniel said. "Dinner's ready."

"It smells delicious!" Caitlin walked around her grandmother's chair and helped her to her feet, suggesting that she could return to the television after they ate. Pam was initially resistant, but she soon allowed herself to be led.

Daniel sat at the head of the table, which felt unnatural to him. Back in the old days, his mother had sat at the head, with Lisa and Daniel on either side— at least until one or both of them had bickered with their mother and fled the table. He sliced the turkey and served it, watching as Aiden played with his yams, smearing his cheeks with orange.

Brent chatted easily about his trip from California, which had begun yesterday evening. He was working online these days, which meant he could remain on the Vineyard all winter long if he wanted to. Caitlin's eyes glinted knowingly. Daniel had a hunch she would bide her time before suggesting they live out here.

Then again, if both Caitlin and Brent worked online, there was no reason they couldn't spend half of their lives on the Vineyard and the other half in California. It was the dawn of a new digital age.

As Daniel feasted, listening to Brent's stories, Caitlin's exclamations, Aiden's squawks, and Pam's occasional outbursts demanding where Lisa was, Daniel allowed himself a brief moment of calm happiness.

But all that ended when the phone rang. It blared ominously from the kitchen, tearing through their family's contentment.

"I'll get it!" Caitlin said.

"No, no. Don't worry. Keep eating," Daniel said as he lurched from the table and into the kitchen. Skillets and pots remained strewn across the stove, a reminder of the tremendous amount of post-dinner cleanup that awaited.

"Bloom residence," Daniel answered, cradling the phone against his ear. "Happy Thanksgiving."

For a long time, there was only silence on the other line. Daniel assumed it was a prank phone call, a mistake.

"Hello?" Daniel asked, his voice spiking with impatience. "Is someone there?"

There was a sharp inhale, followed by a soft cry.

"Hello?" Daniel demanded.

And then, finally: "Daniel? It's me. It's Lisa."

Shackled with the horror of this surprise, Daniel's knees gave out, and he collapsed against the kitchen wall, his heart pounding. It felt as though Lisa called from beyond the grave. And he had no idea what would happen next. What could she possibly want from him? And what did she plan to destroy in their lives next?

Chapter Twenty-Two

T he entire Coleman Family had agreed to meet
at Oriana's home for Thanksgiving that year,
requiring what had seemed to be one hundred
hours of preparation in Oriana's kitchen. Meghan had
been up to her elbows in turkey, pumpkin puree, stuffing,
and butter, frequently pausing to sip wine and crack jokes
with Oriana, who never seemed phased by the onslaught
of work. "It's such a joy to host both sides of the Coleman
Families," she'd said more than once. "I never could have
imagined this last year."

Now, Meghan sat at the massive table, her fingers
laced with her father's as they bent their heads in prayer.
On the other side of Chuck was Oriana, and across from
them were Roland and Grant— the united front of the
Coleman families. Surrounding them were Roland and
Grant's wives, Hugo, Reese, and the rest of the Coleman
members— Roland's children, Grant's children, and all
the grandchildren. Brea, Oriana's once-business partner
and best friend, who had disappeared from their lives for
many years, joined as well, smiling happily on the far end

of the table. It had been nearly impossible to quiet down enough for the prayer. But now, as Chuck thanked God above for bringing them together for this immaculate feast, not a soul made a peep.

"Amen," Chuck broke the prayer and gave Meghan's hand a final squeeze. "Let's eat!"

Meghan laughed, blinking back tears. On the other side of her, Hugo nudged her with his elbow, winking.

"I haven't seen Meghan all week," he announced. "She's been here with Oriana, prepping for this feast."

"I kidnapped her for the week," Oriana affirmed, passing a large bowl of salad down the table. "But we had our fun, didn't we, Meg?"

"Uh oh," Reese said. "Hugo and I know what that means."

"They were up to no good," Hugo agreed. "It's a surprise they got any cooking done at all."

Meghan allowed herself to relax into the chaotic banter of her large family, inhaling the autumnal scents of thick gravy and spiced pumpkin pie. Ever since the island-wide gossip regarding Hugo and his "disappeared" girlfriend, Lisa, her family had banded together for her, frequently calling to ask if she was all right. Oriana had initially demanded, "Why didn't you tell me this was going on!" in a way that suggested anger, but she'd then broken down, telling Meghan she wanted to be there for her every step of the way in life. She'd also reminded Meghan of something she knew to be true beyond a shadow of a doubt: Hugo loved her to pieces. The past didn't matter.

"What's Daniel doing for Thanksgiving today?" Oriana asked over the table, catching Meghan's eye as she scooped herself a serving of candied yams.

"He spent all morning cooking for his daughter, her son, and his mother," Meghan said. "Last year and the one before that, it was just him and his mother for Thanksgiving."

"Pam Bloom is hard work," Chuck said contemplatively, having met her numerous times in the past.

"She's not really herself these days," Meghan said.

Chuck furrowed his brow. "I'm sorry to hear that. Your friend Daniel is a good man, helping out the way he is. It's never easy to care for a sick parent— especially with such a complex history behind you."

Meghan felt a darkness behind her father's words, and she wondered whether he spoke of his own parents, of experiences he'd never shared with her. Chuck's parents had both passed away before Meghan had been born, and she only knew them from photographs and vague stories.

It was incredible, she thought now, what we hid from one another in order to protect ourselves from the truth.

Hugo cupped Meghan's knee with his large hand, filling her with a sense of warmth and belonging. As though to address the gossip that had circulated the island head-on, he said, "Daniel came over for dinner the other night. Gosh, I hadn't seen him in decades."

On the other side of the table, Eva perked up, her eyes glinting with intrigue. With her fork hovering over her plate, she asked, "How did that go?"

Hugo tilted his head thoughtfully. "It was emotional, to say the least. I first met Daniel when he was seven or eight, just a little kid. I watched him grow up, you know? And I genuinely cared for him as though he were my own brother. But the man who came over for dinner the other night was fifty years old! He'd been married; he'd had a child. He'd lived an entire life out in California. In hearing his stories, I took stock of my own, realizing just how grateful I am for everything that's happened." He set his jaw, adding, "I wouldn't change anything."

"It's a privilege, getting older," Chuck said. "At least for me, I only realize how old I am when I look around at everybody else. Look at my daughters! You're fifty and forty-seven? How did that happen? And my sons..." Chuck shook his head as his eyes filled with tears. "I missed so many years of your lives. And I'm so grateful to have you here at my Thanksgiving table, dining with me."

"We get it," Roland joked. "We're older than dirt." Grant chuckled in agreement and raised his glass of wine.

"If you're older than dirt, then what does that make me?" Chuck asked.

"Older than time," Grant answered.

Chuck laughed uproariously, smacking his thigh. Everyone at the table joined, riding the wave of his joy. Even Eva, who, at twenty-six, couldn't possibly fathom what it meant to go through time, laughed wildly, touching Finn's shoulder. In a brief flash of fear, Meghan said a small prayer for Eva and their future. All she wanted in the world was for Eva to enjoy the same happiness Meghan had been allowed. All she wanted was for her children to grow as old and as happy as Chuck.

After dinner, Meghan, Oriana, Brea, Eva, Sam, Hilary, and Estelle cleared the table, wiping away the crumbs to make space for an entire afternoon of pie-eating and conversation. Oriana and Meghan scraped plates into a massive trash can as Estelle breezed in and out of the kitchen to fetch more bottles of wine and brew a pot of coffee. Sam and Hilary started on the dishes, frequently squabbling, as was their way as sisters, and Brea began to slice pie.

"I have to admit," Brea said as she slid a slice of pumpkin onto a china plate. "The island was wild with gossip about you and Hugo, Meghan. It made me nervous."

"You know how this island can be," Oriana said. "It thrives on gossip."

"I was away for so long," Brea offered, speaking of her years in Thailand. "But always, a piece of me wanted to return. It made me wonder about Lisa. If she feels that way, too."

"It's a completely different case," Oriana said. "Lisa was a very broken woman."

"So was I," Brea reminded her.

Oriana reached across the kitchen to touch her best friend's shoulder, a reminder that she was safe with them now. That she'd returned home. That the rest of her life was happening now.

Meghan continued to stack plates, her ears burning with fear. With the coming of Thanksgiving, the "Find Lisa" group had calmed down a little, and there weren't as many "Find Lisa" posters flapping around town. She and Hugo had talked delicately around the topic of Lisa, about what they would do if she ever appeared. Hugo had said he didn't care one way or another— but Meghan didn't fully believe that.

"If she ever comes around here, she'll see that the island has moved on without her," Oriana continued.

Meghan bristled. "I don't think it necessarily has."

"What do you mean?" Oriana asked, her jaw slack.

"Hugo never really moved on, did he? He just tried to delete her from his memories," Meghan went on. "The same could be said for Daniel. Even his mother, Pam, only speaks of Lisa, even this deep into her dementia. Her disappearance really affected everyone. It made it so people couldn't move on, not really, because they always wondered."

Oriana nodded slowly. "You want her to reappear?"

"Maybe it's the best way forward," Meghan whispered. "Honesty. The truth." Her face broke into a nervous smile. "I'm not saying it'll be easy for any of us. And maybe it'll break my heart."

Brea and Oriana held the silence for a moment. The trash bag was full, and Meghan tied the plastic together, her elbows quivering. She hadn't fully realized she'd thought that way, not until she'd said it aloud. It was a marvel what you could reveal to yourself about your inner thoughts. Maybe everyone was a mystery, even to themselves.

Meghan's phone vibrated in her pocket. It was Daniel. "I'll be right back," she said, disappearing into the mudroom and closing the door behind her. She wondered what Oriana and Brea said about her admittance, her desire for truth. Maybe they thought she'd lost her mind.

"Hey! Happy Thanksgiving!"

Daniel's voice wavered. "Hey. Did you already eat?"

"Just finished. You?"

"We finished a little while ago, yeah." He coughed. It sounded as though there was something lodged in his throat. "My daughter's husband came by."

"From California?" Meghan was impressed. "I remember you said you were afraid they were getting divorced."

"They seem happy as clams right now," Daniel said.

"I can hear them laughing from the next room. And Aiden's thrilled to have his daddy back."

"I can only imagine."

Daniel was quiet for a moment. Meghan could feel a darkness upon his heart. For not the first time, she felt guilty that she had her love with Hugo, that she had romantic support. Maybe she could help Daniel with the dating scene? There had to be someone on the island he could build a relationship with. There was always so much love to go around.

But then, Daniel interrupted her reverie. "Do you have any time to meet up this weekend? Maybe Saturday?"

"Saturday's great," Meghan said. "I'm going shopping tomorrow, but I'm free as a bird the rest of the weekend. Want to get some food?" She laughed. "Not that I ever need to eat again after the meal I just had."

"Food sounds okay," Daniel said, still sounding distracted.

Meghan furrowed her brow. "Is there something going on, Daniel?"

"I'm not sure, to be honest. I can explain everything when we see each other," Daniel said. "Enjoy the rest of your holiday, okay?"

After that, he hung up, leaving Meghan alone in the mudroom at Oriana's place, listening as her enormous family bubbled and bantered through the living room, laughing, opening fresh bottles of wine and commenting on the football game. It was impossible to understand what had upset Daniel, what it was he wanted to discuss.

Suddenly, there came a knock at the mudroom door, and Meghan whipped up to open it. Hugo stood in the doorframe, his hair a wild mess of curls, his cheeks pink from overeating and laughing.

"I heard a rumor you were in here," he said. "Do you mind if I come in?"

Meghan took a small step backward, her heart pounding as she was struck with a long-ago memory. During the first Thanksgiving she'd spent with Hugo, she'd been pregnant with Eva— exhausted, her feet swollen and sore, and her appetite confusing. One minute, she'd been starving; the next, she'd been sick. Unable to sit at the dinner table a moment more, she'd scrambled to the second floor of her parent's home and collapsed on her childhood bed, her head pounding with exhaustion. At twenty, it had felt impossible that she was on the verge of becoming a mother herself, especially when surrounded by her fluffy teddy bear, her stuffed dog with the missing eye. Hugo had appeared in the doorway and said just exactly this: "I heard a rumor you were in here. Do you mind if I come in?" He'd spent the next hour rubbing her feet and telling her stories about their future, describing in fantastical details all the miraculous ways their baby would change the world. She'd fallen even deeper in love with him after that.

There in the mudroom of Oriana's home, Meghan rose up on her tiptoes and kissed Hugo with her eyes closed. No matter the storms of gossip or the chaos of what had come before, she and Hugo would find a way to be happy. They always had.

Chapter Twenty-Three

D aniel didn't tell anyone about his plans on the Friday after Thanksgiving. He stood on the dock, his hands shoved deep in his pockets as he watched the ferry draw closer over the dark, surging water. As the vessel dropped its ramp, a few stragglers peeked over the edge of the boat, looking out over an island blanketed with snow. It was impossible to know, from this distance, if any of them was his sister. Perhaps she'd chickened out.

As the crowd descended from the ferry, Daniel tried to make peace with the idea that his sister probably hadn't made it. Over the phone, her voice had been filled with terror, and she'd sounded on the verge of hanging up.

"I heard about a search party," she'd said. "Looking for me? Of all people?"

"That's what happens when you disappear like that," Daniel had said. "People wonder where the heck you went."

Lisa Bloom was the last person to leave the ferry, as though she'd waited in the onboard café, weighing up whether or not she should go. She wore a thick black peacoat, a winter hat, and glasses, and she was slender, shorter than Daniel had remembered. In his mind, she'd become a sort of monster, a woman who'd always been quick with an insult. As she approached him, a smile played out on her lips, and she stopped about two feet away from him, her eyes widening behind her thick frames.

"It's my baby brother," she said as the wind whipped between them and tangled her blonde hair. Daniel realized she probably dyed it. So much time had passed. They were old.

"Hi," Daniel said, unable to trust himself not to break down. He staggered forward and wrapped her in a hug, trying to shove away his resentment. "How was your trip?"

Their hug broke, and Lisa dropped her gaze. "It was complicated. I almost turned back three times."

Daniel laughed gently, appreciating her honesty. "I imagine." He tugged at his hat. "I guess you don't want to go anywhere you might be recognized?"

"Not yet," Lisa said.

"Edgartown okay?"

Daniel led Lisa to his car, where she buckled herself into the passenger side and continued to gawk around her.

"Everything's the same, but at the same time, everything's different," she said. "I can't explain it."

"The island upholds its history," Daniel said. "You know that."

Lisa still hadn't told Daniel where she'd been all these years. As he drove toward the eastern side of the island, they held a silence that wasn't at all comfortable. He glanced her way a few times, spotting no wedding ring. Did she have children? A career?

Daniel parked outside a coffee shop and led Lisa into the cozy interior. Several people sat before scones and croissants, either in preparation for Black Friday shopping or taking a break between stops. They ordered Daniel a black coffee and Lisa a Flat White. In the back corner of the coffee shop, they turned to face the wall to avoid anyone's curious eyes.

Finally, Daniel burst with, "I just can't believe it's you."

Lisa tried to smile. She removed her coat, beneath which she wore a pair of jeans and a practical sweater, and sipped her coffee.

"Where did you hear about the search party?" Daniel asked.

"A friend of mine is on social media," Lisa explained. "And she saw a picture of me circulating. I couldn't believe she recognized me. I haven't looked like that in twenty-seven years."

"You don't look so different," Daniel assured her.

"That's nice." Lisa shrugged. "But I've aged. Everybody does."

Daniel coated his tongue with harsh black coffee. "Where have you been?"

As Lisa sighed, Daniel was assaulted with a memory of being very young and completely enamored with his older sister. He'd followed her around, bent on imitating her every move and every word. Where had he put that love for her? Yet here it was, still lurking in his heart.

"I moved around a lot at first," Lisa admitted. "I felt completely insane, out of my mind. I had no gravity after I left the island, and I took refuge with whoever would have me— until I grew tired of them or got into an argument with them. Men. Female friends. Anyone."

Daniel furrowed his brow, thinking of his grand move to California. He'd immediately met Gina. He'd immediately set up a home.

"I got married when I was thirty," Lisa went on. "He was in real estate, and we had a very comfortable life in Virginia, of all places."

Daniel's lips parted with surprise. He'd never have pictured his sister in Virginia. Even now, as he trained his ears, he could hear the slightest of Southern accents.

"And we had children," Lisa continued, her voice very small.

"You did!"

Lisa nodded, pressing her lips together. "You too?"

"Just one. A daughter."

"I have a niece." Lisa looked captivated and took another sip of her coffee. "My gosh. Name?"

"Caitlin. And she has a son, too. Aiden."

Lisa's eyes widened. "I have— I mean, had— two daughters. Brittany and Rachel."

"Had?"

Lisa dropped her chin. "Rachel died when she was a teenager. Cancer."

Daniel's heart shattered. Without thinking, he reached across the table and took Lisa's hand. He now recognized the grief etched across her face. It wasn't anything she would ever be able to flee.

"It nearly destroyed me, obviously," Lisa went on, speaking to the ground. "My husband and I got divorced shortly afterward. It was just too big of a strain."

"I can understand that."

"Horribly, Brittany moved to the city after that," Lisa

said, her voice breaking. "I was too entrenched in grief to see myself in what she was doing. She didn't want to talk to me. She didn't want to go over and over the memories of her sister. I was so angry with her! I said some things via text that I can never take back."

Daniel's heart seized.

"And I realized Brittany and I were just going over old territory," Lisa continued, her eyes heavy with tears. "I was mean and broken, like Mom. And Brittany was me, just wanting to be free." Lisa puffed out her cheeks and blinked up at a painting of a vase on the wall. "Miraculously, Brittany has started checking up on me lately. She still lives in the city, but she asked me to visit. Gosh, Daniel. I was watching myself get older and more and more lonely. I don't know why my daughter took any mercy on me." She winced. "And then, my friend sent me the flyer with my face on it— a reminder that Brittany wasn't the only one who ran away. I had done the running first. I'd left a mountain of pain here on Martha's Vineyard. I'd always known that, but I'd taught myself not to care. Aren't I a monster?

"It took all the bravery I had to call you yesterday," Lisa whispered. "I never thought for a minute you'd welcome me back with open arms. Yet here you are, listening to me ramble." She paused for a moment. "It's been a long time since someone allowed me to ramble. Even my therapist interjects here and there, demanding that I unpack what I've just said."

Daniel's ears perked up. "You're going to therapy?"

Lisa nodded. "With the divorce, Rachel's death, and Brittany leaving, I realized I couldn't deal with myself anymore. Slowly, my therapist has forced me to take stock of my actions. And it's taken a very long time, but I've finally begun to face what happened twenty-seven years ago. That, and my mommy issues." She placed her face in her hands.

"Pam Bloom was not just our mother," Daniel tried to joke. "She was a volcanic explosion."

"She was in a car accident," Lisa said.

Daniel wet his lips, unsure of how to approach the next thing he had to tell her. "Mom's sick."

The remaining color drained from Lisa's already pale face.

"Dementia," Daniel went on.

"Gosh." Lisa shook her head. "I'm officially speechless."

Daniel gave Lisa the abridged version of the previous few years: that their mother's doctor had called him to say she couldn't live by herself anymore, that Daniel had moved Gina out here as a last-ditch effort to save their marriage and save their mother; that Gina had left and divorced him, leaving him lonelier than he'd ever been. Throughout, Lisa's face hardened with shock.

"I take full responsibility for this," Lisa whispered. "I should have been here."

Daniel, in all his years of knowing his sister, had never known her to take full responsibility. He swallowed the lump in his throat.

Lisa took Daniel's hand across the table and went on. "I'm here now, Daniel. I don't have anything back in Virginia. I don't even have a pet."

Daniel chortled with surprise laughter and blinked back tears.

"There is no reason you should forgive me for leaving you like that," Lisa whispered. "But I'm willing to work for your forgiveness if you'll have me."

Daniel shook his head, at a loss. Never in a million years had he imagined this.

"I don't want you to go away again," he said simply, feeling like the little boy he'd always been. "I want us to be a family."

"I need a family," Lisa said, her eyes widening. "So much more than I ever knew."

Chapter Twenty-Four

Meghan was cozy in bed Saturday morning, listening to the soft rush of water against the porcelain shower. Hugo had woken up early to go for a long run, ten full miles, and his plan was to get cleaned up, brew them coffee, and bring Meghan breakfast in bed. Outside, an eggshell blue sky swelled overhead, and there was a chirping of birds somewhere along the coast. The darkness of the previous weeks was long gone. Meghan was happier than ever.

When Hugo appeared with the breakfast tray, Meghan shifted up to lean on three plush pillows. Upon the tray were fresh strawberries, fried eggs, crisp bacon, and beautiful croissants, a scrumptious array. Hugo leaned over the tray and kissed Meghan first on the lips, then on the cheek.

"You look happy," Meghan said.

"Running endorphins!" Hugo laughed and stretched out his long, muscular legs. In just his boxers and a t-shirt, he looked like a guy in a Hanes commercial. "That, and I get to spend this beautiful morning with my beautiful wife."

"Stop buttering me up," Meghan joked, taking a strawberry.

"I'm just telling the truth," Hugo assured her, beaming with love.

After breakfast, Meghan showered and dressed in a pair of jeans and a dark red sweater. She and Daniel had arranged to meet at one at the bookstore, at which time Daniel's employee planned to take over for the afternoon to allow Daniel some more time off. Meghan was proud of Daniel for making more time for himself and his personal needs. Still, she had no idea what he wanted to talk about. When she'd texted him yesterday about something inane she'd read in the news, he hadn't answered, which wasn't like him. Was there something wrong?

Meghan kissed Hugo goodbye and headed out a little before one, her heart beating a little too quickly. On the drive, she tried to train her breathing, counting four beats for the inhale and four for the exhale. Nothing worked.

The bookstore was bustling, with a line snaking from the register all the way to the fantasy section. Meghan snuck between two young families, eyes to the corners for some sign of Daniel. His employee helmed the counter, making small talk with islanders, ensuring they felt a part of The White Whale Bookstore family.

Because she'd done it so many times, Meghan easily snuck behind the counter to find Daniel in his office, staring at the wall. He wore a strange expression, his cheeks gray. When he heard her, he leaped from his chair, making it swivel.

"Meghan! Hey." He palmed the back of his neck.

"Hey. You okay?" Meghan couldn't breathe. To her, Daniel looked very ill, on the brink of collapse.

"I'm fine. It's just been an interesting weekend, to say the least."

Meghan shifted her weight. "Do you still want to get lunch?"

"I don't know if I can eat," Daniel answered, returning to his chair and staring at the wall again. "And I really don't know how to tell you what happened."

"You're killing me, Daniel," Meghan breathed. "Help me out here."

Daniel nodded, wetting his lips and taking an enormous breath. "Lisa's on the island."

Meghan felt the weight of his words crash into her, and she nearly fell to her knees. It took all her strength to keep herself upright. "When did she get here?"

"She called on Thanksgiving," Daniel explained, "and said she was at the airport. She'd already bought a ticket to Boston. But she told me to tell her if I didn't want her to come."

"She put that in your hands?"

"She didn't want to barge back into my life if I didn't want her," Daniel said. "Which I appreciate."

Meghan crossed her arms tightly over her chest, feeling as though she floated above the earth, looking down upon it. "The search party got to her?"

"Her friend saw the flyer circulating online," Daniel said.

"Wow."

Daniel sighed and forced his eyes back to Meghan's.

"This must be such an intense time for you," Meghan hurried to say.

"It is, and it isn't," Daniel offered, adjusting his collar. "She's been through so much."

"So have you," Meghan pointed out.

Daniel raised his shoulders. "She lost her daughter. Cancer."

Now, Meghan really did need to sit down. She collapsed on the only other chair in the room, where her knees knocked together. "That's horrible, Daniel."

"We spent all day yesterday talking," Daniel said. "I've never felt closer to my sister in my life. We poured our hearts out to one another."

"That's beautiful."

Daniel furrowed his brow. "I never imagined I would ever find a way to forgive her. But she's been through years of therapy at this point. She sees everything she was, along with where she got it from. But more than that, she doesn't blame my mother, either."

"Generational trauma," Meghan breathed.

"It's unavoidable," Daniel agreed. "Although I've done my best not to pass it on."

They were quiet. Out in the bookstore, a little girl shrieked with excitement over a series of princess chapter books as her mother assured her she could have the first three.

"I want to build this relationship with my sister," Daniel said quietly. "But I don't want it to ruin my friendship with you."

Meghan was moved at the tenderness in Daniel's face. "Daniel, you can't do anything because of me."

Daniel set his jaw. "The past few weeks have changed my life, Meghan. It's because of our friendship that Lisa found her way back to the Vineyard at all. I can't help but think it all happened for a reason."

Meghan stared outside, her ears thudding with the strength of her heartbeat. "Did she say anything about Hugo?"

"She did."

Meghan's throat nearly closed. "What did she say?" Meghan could only think of the worst possible things: that Lisa regretted leaving Hugo, that Hugo had been her greatest love.

"She wants to apologize to him," Daniel offered. "And when I told her about you, she wept."

Meghan closed her eyes.

"But not because she was jealous," Daniel hurried to add. "She said she was relieved. She hated how she treated Hugo over the years, and she was so happy he'd gone on to find love and happiness with you."

Meghan's tears flowed freely so that the office around her blurred, colors morphing together. After a long time, during which her breathing was ragged, and her thoughts were not entirely kind, she heard herself speak.

"You should come over for dinner. Both of you."

Daniel furrowed his brow. "Are you sure, Meghan?"

"I'm not sure about much of anything," Meghan offered. "But two things I am sure about are you and Hugo. You're two of the most important people in my life. And Lisa is important to both of you. I want to meet her. And I want Hugo to hear what she has to say. He deserves it."

Chapter Twenty-Five

The days leading up to the dinner with Lisa were frayed at the edges. Meghan slept fitfully, frequently waking up in the middle of the night to stare down at Hugo's sleeping form. It was as though her unconscious mind demanded she make sure everything was just as she'd left it, that Lisa hadn't swooped in and taken everything she loved. It wasn't rational, but love never was.

Hugo was similarly panicked. His long runs grew longer until he often spent two hours out on the trails, pounding his feet into a rhythm that, he said, blocked out his fears.

But the difference between now and a month ago was this: Hugo and Meghan actually discussed what they were going through. Night after night, they sat at the kitchen table, shared a bottle of wine, and talked about the positives and negatives of what they were about to do. Once or twice, Hugo had even suggested they call off the dinner, pretend that Lisa wasn't on the island at all, and move on with their lives. But each time, Meghan had reminded him: with honesty and openness, they could find freedom, both with one another and each other. Lisa didn't matter anymore, not really— but she once had. Like it or not, Lisa was a part of Meghan and Hugo's story.

"I couldn't tell you were so broken-hearted when we met. I wish I had known." Meghan sat cross-legged at the kitchen table, swirling a Primitivo in her glass as snowflakes melted against the windowpane.

"I masked it from everyone," Hugo admitted. Meghan was grateful he didn't point out this was their twelfth conversation about this very topic in the previous few days. He'd told her: *whatever you want to say, say it as many times as you need.*

"I was so inexperienced back then," Meghan said. "I'd had that high school boyfriend."

"The one you didn't even like?"

Meghan giggled into her wine glass so that it echoed before she took a sip. "I had this belief that the minute I met 'the one,' I would know."

"I take it you didn't feel that with your high school ex?"

Meghan shook her head and touched Hugo's hand across the table. "But when I saw you on the other side of that party..."

"You thought to yourself, 'I should throw my beer at that guy.'"

Meghan chortled. "Exactly."

Hugo exhaled deeply, his eyes warm and soft from his first glass of wine, his posture slumped after a fifteen-mile run. "I knew, too. When I saw you, I mean."

"How could you have known? I mean, you and Lisa had just broken up."

"It was a gut feeling," Hugo said quietly. "One I had

never had with Lisa." He palmed the back of his neck and studied the snow outside. Behind that was inky darkness, save for a smattering of stars above a colossal ocean. "Lisa had just always been there. We'd gotten close immediately. You know Martha's Vineyard. People marry their high school sweethearts here. I figured we were meant for that, too. I didn't question it. And then, I met the sort of woman who questions everything."

"Me?"

"You." His eyes were narrow. "You carved out space for yourself within an industry that's usually exclusively male. You dumped your high school boyfriend because he bored you. You did everything you wanted to do every step of the way. I was in love with that from the very beginning." He squeezed her hand, teasing her. "Now, admit it. You just fell in love with my good looks."

"I'm shallow," Meghan quipped. "What can I say?" But a moment later, she'd abandoned her chair and swallowed him in a hug, feeling the firm thump of his heartbeat through her entire body. Although her eyes watered with fear for what approached, she felt stronger than ever in what they'd built. It was a foundation.

She couldn't believe she'd spent a couple of weeks doubting it.

* * *

On the day of the dinner with Lisa, Meghan and Hugo both quit working by two and went grocery shopping. They were bent on providing the kind of dinner that, given the awkward circumstances, was at least good enough to fill an hour's worth of conversation. Meghan imagined Lisa to be blonde and approximately twenty-five years old, which she knew was incorrect. She also imagined her gushing about the dinner Meghan and Hugo cooked, as though it represented the depth of the connection Hugo and Meghan had.

After Meghan and Hugo returned home with ingredients for enough clam chowder, fresh biscuits, and Brussels sprouts to feed a small army, they set to work, slicing and dicing and filling the house with smells Meghan could only describe as "cozy."

As the soup bubbled and spat in the large pot, Meghan poured them glasses of wine and rubbed the top of Hugo's shoulder. It was stiff as a board and hardly gave to her touch.

"Oh, baby," Meghan breathed, sensing his anxiety. She kissed his bicep. "It's going to be okay."

Hugo's forehead crumpled together. "I can't stop thinking about all the bad times, you know? It's like, as she gets closer and closer to our home, all I can hear are the horrible things she said to me."

Meghan thought she understood. It was like abuse of any kind lived on in your cells, ready to activate again the minute the abuser returned. Slowly, she turned Hugo toward her and burrowed her head against his chest.

"Do you remember the day Eva was born?' she asked quietly.

"I could never forget that."

"You remember how they took her down the hallway to clean her up," Meghan continued, "and they came back to tell us there was a problem. That she wasn't breathing properly."

Hugo shook in her arms, falling through the memories.

"It didn't take long before she was okay," Meghan

went on. "They were the worst thirty minutes of my life, but we got through them. And then, after they brought her into our room, you held her. I remember thinking that your hands were almost too big for such a little doll, and your eyes were as big as dinner plates. Do you remember what you told her?"

Hugo's eyes glistened with tears. "That I would protect her every single day of her life."

Meghan nodded. "And you have. And you've protected me." Her voice broke, and she hurried to pull herself together again if only to make her point. "Now, it's my turn to protect you. I'll be right by your side throughout this dinner. And the minute you feel uncomfortable, all you have to do is squeeze my hand, and I'll make an excuse and end the dinner immediately. No questions asked."

Just as Hugo lowered his chin, the front doorbell blared. Meghan's stomach tied itself into knots, and she wavered on her feet. A part of her wanted to run. But she'd promised Hugo she would be by his side— and he needed closure. Heck, they all did.

Hugo and Meghan walked hand-in-hand toward the front door. There was an eerie silence on the other side, as though Daniel and Lisa stood with their own sense of doom. Meghan and Hugo locked eyes and inhaled deeply, then turned the handle.

Upon their stoop were Daniel and a woman in her fifties who had similar features. She had bottle-blonde hair, a thick hat, and a black peacoat, and she wore sensible boots with double-tied laces. Her eyes were blue and stunning, but she was also mostly just the same as everyone else.

Almost immediately, Lisa lost the mystique she'd held in Meghan's mind. Meghan's hospitality instincts took over, and she spoke first, breaking the silence.

"Welcome to our home." She caught Lisa's eye and smiled. "And welcome back to the Vineyard."

Daniel and Lisa followed Meghan and Hugo into the foyer. There, Daniel and Meghan stood back as Hugo and Lisa bowed their heads at one another and extended their arms for an awkward hug. Although the sight of her husband hugging his previous love felt a bit like a stab in the belly, Meghan gripped Daniel's arm and reminded herself of everything she'd learned about love that week.

She also said, "Daniel, this is the first time you've been here, right?"

Daniel's smile was crooked, handsome, and far more alive than it had been when she'd first encountered him at that wine bar all those weeks ago. He would meet someone to fall in love with soon, she thought, with or without her help. And she would adore watching him find happiness again.

"This is a gorgeous house," Lisa said to Hugo as she removed her hat and laughed nervously.

"Yeah! We like it." Hugo rubbed his hair and looked at Meghan. "We moved here when?"

"Twenty-four years ago," Meghan informed him, ready to declare every minute of their very long history.

"Right after the birth of our second child," Hugo told Lisa.

"Those must be them." Lisa pointed at a hung photograph of Theo and Eva on the nearest wall, Theo in braces and Eva wearing a collared shirt cut in a style that had gone out long ago. Eva had begged Meghan to change the photograph, if only because she hated the clothes and the pimple on her chin, but Meghan adored the picture. It was practically an antique.

"Quite a while ago," Hugo admitted. "They were sixteen and fourteen there."

"They're beautiful," Lisa said.

"Would anyone like a glass of wine?" Meghan led them into the living room, where the scents from the clam chowder were dense and nourishing. She poured everyone glasses of whatever they liked, with Lisa opting for chardonnay and Daniel and Hugo going for robust reds. Meghan poured a white for herself, terrified of staining her teeth in front of her husband's ex. Vanity had a time and place, she thought.

The night started the only way it could: it was clunky. Lisa talked about her flight from Virginia, her love for Aiden, and her new friendship with Caitlin, her niece. "I can't wait till she meets my daughter, Brittany," she explained. "Brittany is a little bit younger than she is, but not much. And they look so similar!" Lisa pulled out her phone to show a photograph of herself and Brittany on Lisa's most recent trip to the city. "We're repairing our relationship," Lisa said quietly, mostly to Hugo. "It's a process, to say the least."

"Every relationship is always changing," Hugo offered. "You have to stay on your toes."

"I'm learning that," Lisa said, giving Daniel a knowing look.

Dinner was ready not long after that. The four of them sat at the dining room table, spooning the thick clam-filled soup and scraping biscuits through the white sauce. Lisa talked about Virginia, about how different the recipes were down there, and Hugo commented on her new Southern accent.

"I told you!" Daniel cried. "It's funny, isn't it? She sounds like a Southern Belle."

"I do not." Lisa rolled her eyes. "Although my husband was related to a very big Southern family. Maybe I took on some of their attributes."

"I'll say," Hugo teased.

It struck Meghan, as she spooned herself another helping of clam chowder, that Hugo and Daniel treated Lisa the same. It was almost as though Hugo was meeting a long-lost cousin again, with a mountain of shared history that no longer really mattered. With each second that passed, Meghan breathed easier. She even found herself asking Lisa questions about living in Virginia and raising her daughters there. Of course, Meghan had shared with Hugo the news of Lisa's daughter's cancer, but Lisa told an abridged story, explaining that her death had shattered her family. "I've been doing a lot of soul-searching since then," she explained. "So, imagine my surprise when Martha's Vineyard had supposedly sent out a search party for me! My first thought was: yep, I'm lost. I'm so lost."

Hugo shook his head, his face echoing his empathy. And at that moment, Meghan thought she'd never loved him more.

After Meghan cleared their plates, she returned to the table, where Lisa folded her hands daintily over the table-cloth. "I can't thank you both enough for having me over tonight," she said, acknowledging Meghan briefly before returning her eyes to Hugo's. "I have had so much time to think over the years. More than that, I started going to therapy and recognizing my terrible relationship patterns." She swallowed, her eyes swimming with tears.

"Hugo, when we were children, we were in love. And it was one of the nicest things I knew."

Hugo nodded, his Adam's apple bouncing.

"Our lives weren't easy," Lisa went on. "Our mother was cruel, and I learned to be crueler than she ever was. But Hugo, you never deserved my cruelty. And when I left like that, I have to admit that I was trying to teach you and everyone else a lesson. That's ironic, isn't it? Because ultimately, I was learning a lesson myself. I had to force myself into the world. I had to figure out who I was. And I'm still on that journey."

Hugo smiled gently. Beside him, Meghan's heart thudded dangerously loudly, and she told herself to breathe. This was why Lisa had come. This was clearing the air.

"I am so glad you and Meghan have gone on to have such a wonderful life," Lisa whispered, her voice breaking. "I don't expect anything from you. Not your friendship, nor your forgiveness. I just wanted to come here tonight and tell you that you were never far from my mind as I officially 'grew up' in Virginia. And I always knew I treated you terribly."

Hugo bowed his head, on the verge of tears. "I can't thank you enough for saying that." After a dramatic pause, he turned to face Meghan and reached for her hand. "Please know that you have friends in us whenever you need them."

Lisa's smile was hesitant. "I'm planning to stay on the Vineyard for a little while, at least. My mother needs help, and it's not fair to Daniel to take on all the work." She eyed him, rolling her shoulders back, and it was as though the tension in the air had cleared. "Besides. Danny and I are both divorced now. It's like we're teenagers all over again. Time to get back in the dating pool, huh, little brother?"

Daniel's cheeks were ruby. "You should see how out of practice I am. That's the only reason Meghan and I met!"

Lisa turned her head so that her cerulean eyes were directly at Meghan. They were staggeringly intense, so much so that Meghan forgot to breathe.

"I'm so glad you and my brother became friends," she said. "You must be a truly extraordinary woman. I'd love to get to know you better."

Meghan was moved. In a flash of unreality, she realized she'd hardly ever considered what Lisa must think of her, the woman who'd stepped up to date her recent ex so soon after she'd gone. It seemed proof of her maturity that she was here today, respecting Meghan herself and the world she'd built with Hugo.

Thankfully, to ease Meghan's cortisol levels and ever-present anxiety, Lisa and Daniel didn't stay long. They didn't like leaving Caitlin and Brent too long with their mother, who often bickered with them, thinking them to be too young to take care of her. As a united front, they stood up, saying no to dessert, and hugged Meghan and Hugo goodbye. During Meghan's hug with Daniel, she squeezed him extra hard and insisted, "We're meeting at the wine bar soon, whether you like it or not." Daniel winked as they parted. "I'll be there."

After Daniel's car disappeared around the curve of the long, coastal road, Meghan turned to Hugo in the foyer and collapsed against him. They held one another for a long time, listening to the surge of the winter wind outside. It had been a horrifically complex, emotional time. But in meeting Lisa, they'd cleared the air.

With quiet certainty, Hugo piled the dried logs from the felled tree limb into the fireplace and made a fire. Meghan was cozied up on the couch in front of him, watching his muscles flicker beneath his long-sleeved t-shirt. How had she gotten so lucky to meet this man?

As the flames licked the sturdy wood, crawling up the sides of the stone basin, Meghan burrowed her head against Hugo's chest. They were forty-seven and fifty-two years old, inching toward old age in a way that both frightened and thrilled her. How wonderful to have gone through so much life with someone! How wonderful to face every obstacle together.

"Do you think she'll be okay?" Meghan broke the silence, thinking again of Lisa, of all she'd lost.

"She's on her way there," Hugo said. "That's all anyone can hope for, isn't it?" He laughed gently and kissed her cheek. "Except for us, of course. It seems to me we've almost always been okay. Almost. Except for the last couple of weeks."

Meghan winced. "I promise I'll come to you first the next time I'm not okay."

"You better, Meghan Coleman," Hugo said.

Meghan pressed her nose against his just as another surge of snow and wind blasted against the house, coming off the Vineyard Sound. "Do you have any more secrets up your sleeves, Hugo Porter?"

"You officially know it all," Hugo told her. "You?"

Meghan gave him a coy smile. As she gazed at him, her mind's eye filled with an onslaught of gorgeous memories— all of which became a patchwork of her life. All of it had been possible with his love.

"I guess you'll have to stick around to find out," Meghan teased, leaning forward to drop her lips against his. There, in the flickering glow of the fire, they held each other close, bolstered with their memories and optimistic enough to hope for thousands more. It was winter on Martha's Vineyard, less than a month till Christmas—and, side-by-side, they were ready for whatever happened next. No matter what.

Coming Next

Pre Order Heart of Christmas

Other Books by Katie Winters

Made in the USA
Middletown, DE
06 September 2024

60515558R00119